* *

SOMEONE
ELSE'S
SHOES

* *

SOMEONE ELSE'S SHOES

ELLEN WITTLINGER

ini Charlesbridge

For David, for forty-odd years.

And for every comedian who has ever made me
forget, even briefly, how heartbreaking life can be.

Published by Charlesbridge
85 Main Street
Watertown, MA 02472
(617) 926-0329
www.charlesbridge.com

Library of Congress Cataloging-in-Publication Data
Names: Wittlinger, Ellen, author.
Title: Someone else's shoes / Ellen Wittlinger.
Description: Watertown, MA: Charlesbridge, [2018] |
Summary: Twelve-year-old Izzy's life just seems to get more and more complicated: she
is upset by her father's new marriage, and a new baby on the way; she is expected to
look out for her ten-year-old cousin, Oliver, who has moved in with her family since his
mother committed suicide, because his father is depressed and having trouble coping;
and now Ben, the rebellious sixteen-year-old son of Izzy's mother's boyfriend, is also
living with them--but when Oliver's father disappears, the three children put aside
their differences and set out to find him.
Identifiers: LCCN 2017057210 (print) | LCCN 2017059484 (ebook) |
ISBN 9781607349952 (ebook) | ISBN 9781580897495 (reinforced for library use)
Subjects: LCSH: Families—Juvenile fiction. | Broken homes—Juvenile fiction. |
Depression, Mental—Juvenile fiction. | Cousins—Juvenile fiction. |
Missing persons—Juvenile fiction. | Friendship—Juvenile fiction. |
CYAC: Family life—Fiction. | Divorce—Fiction. | Depression, Mental—Fiction.|
Cousins—Fiction. | Missing persons—Fiction. | Friendship—Fiction.
Classification: LCC PZ7.W78436 (ebook) | LCC PZ7.W78436 So 2018 (print) |
DDC 813.54 [Fic]—dc23
LC record available at https://lccn.loc.gov/2017057210

Printed in the United States of America
(hc) 10 9 8 7 6 5 4 3 2 1

Display type set in Lunchbox Slab by Kimmy Design
Text type set in New Century Schoolbook
Printed by Berryville Graphics in Berryville, Virginia, USA
Production supervision by Brian G. Walker
Designed by Sarah Richards Taylor

We look before and after,
And pine for what is not;
Our sincerest laughter
With some pain is fraught;
Our sweetest songs are those
    that tell of saddest thought.

—Percy Bysshe Shelley

* *

CHAPTER 1

"Why are you running?" Oliver called to her.

"Why are you such a slowpoke?" Izzy answered.

Lately a small, gloomy shadow followed Izzy Shepherd everywhere she went. His name was Oliver Hook, and he was her cousin. Marching through downtown Coolidge, Izzy was at least three strides ahead of the kid.

"Are you running away from me?" Oliver yelled.

"*No.*" Of course she wasn't running away from him. But a little pinprick of guilt made her slow down anyway. "I don't see why I have to go with

"I never bought a pair of shoes by myself," Oliver said.

Izzy stopped walking and turned to stare at him. "You're ten years old, and you've never bought a pair of shoes by yourself?"

"That's not weird. My mom always went with me. You always try to make me sound weird, Izzy."

"It's not that hard to do," she mumbled, hoping that Oliver couldn't actually hear her. It wasn't his fault he was suddenly her responsibility. She knew it wasn't fair to take it out on him. She was really mad at the grown-ups, but they had so much else going on, they didn't even notice.

The sun bounced off the storefront windows, hit the sidewalk, and exploded into her face. She'd forgotten her sunglasses, and the dazzling light made her squint. All around her, people were rolling up their sleeves to enjoy the end-of-summer sun on their skin, but Izzy could feel the approach of autumn racing toward her, and she hunched her shoulders against it. She didn't like change. In her experience, it never made things better.

What was this, now? Some guy in baggy trousers, a striped shirt, and bright red lips on a white-painted face zigzagged through traffic and hopped onto the sidewalk behind Oliver. He wore white gloves and a big black hat and had red circles painted on his cheeks. Oliver wasn't paying attention, but Izzy caught the movement out of the corner of her eye and turned to watch the man dragging his feet in obvious imitation of her cousin.

Ugh, he must be a mime from the festival in the park. Why did people think mimes were funny, anyway? Nobody appreciated comedy more than Izzy, but she liked humor to come from words and ideas, not imitation. Mimes just exaggerated everything that was odd or silly about a person. That wasn't funny—it was mean.

"Stop following us!" she yelled at the guy. "You look ridiculous!"

Oliver turned too, surprised to see the clownish figure. He smiled briefly, and the mime returned the same smile.

"He's making fun of you," Izzy hissed, and then sped up again, hoping Oliver would too.

"Why would he do that?" Oliver asked.

"Because that's what mimes do!"

The man passed Oliver so that he occupied the space on the sidewalk between the two cousins. His shoulders pulled back and his neck stiffened as he matched Izzy's aggravated gait.

Oliver's sudden, barking laugh surprised Izzy. She hadn't heard a sound like that the entire three weeks the kid had been staying at her house. "He's walking just like you do!" Oliver said. "Like you're trying to get away from something."

Izzy put on the brakes so fast, the mime ran into her. "Go away!" she yelled at him. He shrugged and began to immediately follow a woman walking in the opposite direction. She had a big handbag over one arm, and he leaned to the right with the weight of it, just like she did.

"Who is that guy?" Oliver asked. "He's pretty funny."

"I don't think so. All kinds of nutballs are hanging around the park this week, pretending to be artists." If Oliver thought that guy was funny, Izzy would have to show him some of her DVDs. Wait till he saw Robin Williams as Mrs. Doubtfire.

"We don't have stuff like this where I live," he said. "Our town's too little."

"You're lucky." But then, because Izzy knew good and well that Oliver was certainly *not* lucky, she felt embarrassed and steered the conversation back around to herself. "Just because I'm a natural leader," she said, "doesn't mean I want to be followed by somebody." Maybe her cousin would get that she didn't only mean the mime.

"Here," she said, turning in to the shoe store. She held the door open while Oliver dragged his fingers along the window glass, ogling the merchandise. "Come on!"

She'd never felt impatient with Oliver before—not until he and his dad had moved into her house.

But Izzy thought it was better to feel annoyed with him than to feel sorry for him. Nobody wanted that, did they? In Izzy's experience, pity made you feel like a mangy dog that people might throw some food at but certainly didn't want to touch.

Inside the store, Izzy's attention was captured by a pair of pretty ballerina flats that came in lots of colors, including a sparkly silver. The silver shoe on display was just her size, so she slipped it on and admired the way it made her ankle look long and slim. If only her mother had given her enough money to get herself a pair of shoes too, but she hadn't.

Izzy needed new school shoes—her toes were squished in her old sneakers and the soles were coming loose. In fact, none of her old shoes fit right anymore—her feet must have grown over the summer. But her mother had hardly listened when Izzy had told her about her shoe requirements. All her mother seemed to have time for these days was worrying about her brother— Izzy's uncle Henderson—and Oliver. Apparently there was a rule that if your mother was a nurse, she had to help everybody else on earth before she had time to listen to *your* problems.

Oliver stood in front of her, holding a very ugly pair of brown sneakers with Velcro straps across the front.

"I like these," he said.

"Are you kidding? Only babies wear Velcro."

"That's not true."

Izzy blew out a stream of exasperated air. "You're starting a new school next week, Oliver. You want the kids to think you're cool, don't you?"

"How can shoes be cool? They're just shoes."

"Also," she continued, "don't tuck your shirt in so tight. It makes you look nerdy."

Oliver shrugged. "I don't care what anybody thinks. We're probably not staying in Coolidge that long anyway."

Izzy hoped he was right about that, but she had her doubts. She found a pair of the kind of shoes boys were supposed to wear. Black high-tops with fat laces. When a salesman came over, she handed him the sample. "We need these in a size six."

"But I don't like laces," Oliver said. "They come open."

"God, Oliver, you're going into fifth grade. You can tie your shoes, can't you?"

"You're so bossy!" he said, but she could tell he was giving up the fight.

Am I bossy? Izzy wondered. Is it bossy if you're just helping somebody for their own good? Ten minutes later they left the store with the high-tops in a box.

"I hear music," Oliver said as they walked out

of the shopping district toward Izzy's house. "Can we go listen?"

Izzy groaned. "There'll be a million people in the park."

"You always exaggerate. Maybe a hundred."

They might as well go to the park. As soon as they got home, Izzy's mother would just come up with some other boring task that fell under the heading of "being extra kind to Oliver these days." She'd ask Izzy to "rise to the occasion," as if she hadn't been doing that for weeks already. Izzy was quite sure that being extra kind to her cousin wasn't going to make a bit of difference to him anyway. Not six weeks ago Oliver's mother had killed herself, which was about the worst thing that could happen to a kid. Nothing anybody could do for him was going to change that.

Izzy felt bad for Oliver—how could she not? But his problem was so enormous and overwhelming, there wasn't any room left for anyone to care about her smaller troubles, which didn't feel all that small to her.

They stood in the sparse circle that surrounded the guitar player, a middle-aged man wearing cowboy boots and a trucker hat. He could strum his instrument well enough, but his raspy voice grated on Izzy's last nerve. Man, she thought, they let anybody play here.

Oliver wasn't impressed either. "My dad's a lot better than that guy," he said as they left the park.

"Well, *yeah*," Izzy said. "Your dad's a professional." Or he *was*, anyway.

"I wish Dad would play his guitar again," Oliver said. "He hasn't even touched it since . . . you know."

"My mom says not to rush him. He'll start performing again eventually."

Izzy didn't actually hold out much hope for Uncle Henderson resuming his career as a singer-songwriter anytime soon. The man had barely even left the bedroom her mom had assigned him when he and Oliver moved into their big, creaky old house three weeks ago. He didn't play his guitar. He didn't sing. He just sat in the rocking chair and stared out the window, as if his dead wife were likely to come walking up the front sidewalk any minute.

It was awful to say, but Izzy hadn't been that surprised when she heard about Aunt Felicia taking the pills. Aunt Felicia had always spooked Izzy a little bit. She was quiet and nervous—just the opposite of Uncle Henderson—and when she smiled, it never seemed like a *real* smile, but more like a mask she didn't want anyone to see behind. Izzy's mother said that Aunt Felicia's depression was an illness, and that mental illness was not that different from physical illness. She said Aunt Felicia wasn't just sad—it was a lot worse than that—but Izzy still didn't really understand it. She'd had a great husband, a smart little kid, and a job she liked as a gardener. Why wasn't that enough to make her happy?

Izzy was not a psychologist like that Cassie Clayton woman her mother had made her see for a while, but she was twelve years old, and she knew plenty. For one thing, she knew there was no point being overprotective of Oliver just because a bad thing had happened to him. Izzy knew that life could be hard, and sometimes you were going to get hurt. A person needed to toughen up to be able to stand it. That's what she'd had to do when her dad left, and she intended to teach her cousin to toughen up too.

"Izzy?" Oliver said shyly, cocking his head. "When we get home, will you swing me in the hammock?"

She sighed. Her job was not going to be easy.

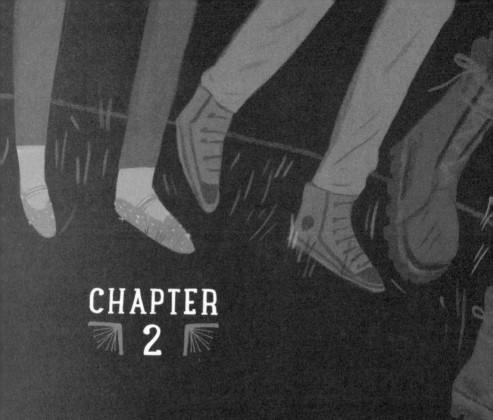

CHAPTER 2

Izzy and Oliver walked up the sagging front steps of her house to find her mother and Ms. Baldwin drinking iced tea on the front porch while Ms. Baldwin's son, Liam, sat cross-legged on the floor, yelling at a handheld video game.

"There you two are!" Izzy's mother said. "Did you get shoes? Let me see."

Oliver handed her the bag, keeping his back to Liam.

"Look, Liam," Ms. Baldwin said. "Oliver's here." Liam grunted and kept poking away at his game.

His mother tried again. "Put that thing down and come say hello to Oliver." Liam ignored her.

Yeah, this was going as well as it had the last time her mother had masterminded a playdate between these two. Izzy wondered how her mother could be so dense. Just because Liam was Oliver's age and also headed for fifth grade at Hopkins Elementary didn't mean the two of them were going to like each other. You could tell just by looking at them that they had nothing in common. Liam's hair was completely buzzed off, and he was wearing a Patriots football jersey three sizes too big, whereas her cousin wore a T-shirt with a picture of SpongeBob SquarePants on it and had that smelly, little-boy hair that stuck up all over his head. Didn't these women have eyes?

Izzy went inside to get herself a glass of tea and find a book to read. By the time she headed back to the porch, Liam and Oliver had been talked into playing in the room her mother called the parlor, a room new houses didn't have because, really, nobody knew what to use it for. Izzy glanced in to see them dumping Oliver's big box of Lego pieces all over the floor. So far, so good.

The front porch was large, and it wrapped around the corner of the house, so Izzy snuggled into a chair on the side of the porch where the women couldn't see her. She opened her book and read the first paragraph, then read it again. It was hard to concentrate when her mother and Ms. Baldwin were speaking in such quiet voices. Obviously they didn't want her to hear, which made Izzy want to listen twice as much. She noticed that if she closed her eyes, her hearing became extra sharp.

"I'm trying to get Henderson to talk to a therapist, but he just ignores me," Izzy's mother said. "It breaks my heart to see my brother in so much pain. And Oliver too, of course. He's being so good, but I know he's scared senseless. He wakes up with nightmares almost every night."

He did? Izzy must have slept through the noise.

"Well, they're fortunate to have you to help them," Ms. Baldwin said.

"I've always felt responsible for Henderson," Izzy's mother said. "He's my younger brother, and after our parents died, he relied on me. We've always been close."

"Is poor Oliver seeing a therapist?" Ms. Baldwin's voice was sickeningly sweet. Izzy could feel her teeth grinding as Ms. Baldwin said "poor."

"We have an appointment with Cassie Clayton next week. She's wonderful with children."

Izzy wouldn't have said Cassie was wonderful. The woman was nice enough, but all that talking had just made Izzy feel worse.

"I don't understand it. How could your sister-in-law do this to such an adorable little boy who needs her so much?" Ms. Baldwin whispered dramatically.

"When you're as sick as Felicia was, you can't think about anything but your own pain," Izzy's mother said. "Her despair lifted sometimes, but never for long. Poor Hen was so hopeful after she came home from the treatment center. She seemed better this time, but it didn't last."

Izzy could hear the ice cubes clink as the women swirled them in their glasses.

"She took pills?"

"Cleaned out the medicine cabinet and swallowed everything in it, including two half-empty bottles of cough medicine. Henderson was out at a gig, and Oliver was asleep in the other room."

These were details Izzy hadn't heard before. She was careful not to move a muscle so as not to remind them she was there.

"Oh my God. The child didn't see anything, did he?"

"I don't think so. Henderson found Felicia when he got home. Oliver woke up when the ambulance got there, but a neighbor came over and took him to her house. I'm sure he knew, though. He's a smart kid. I'm sure he knew immediately."

There was a long silence then, but Izzy couldn't go back to her book. She'd been to Oliver's house lots of times. It wasn't large like the old monstrosity she lived in. Oliver's room was right across the hall from his parents' room. If he'd woken up when he heard the ambulance, he must have seen *something*, and Izzy's imagination was able to come up with many possibilities. He must have seen his father wailing and sobbing in the middle of the night. He must have seen the paramedics race in with life-saving equipment they wouldn't need. Maybe, before that neighbor hurried him away, he even saw his mother's body with nobody left inside anymore. Imagining it made Izzy feel sick to her stomach.

"That poor, poor baby!" Ms. Baldwin sounded like she was about to start bawling herself. "This is going to ruin his whole life!"

What was that woman talking about? Izzy smacked her book down on the floor and stomped around the corner to confront the two women. "First of all, Oliver is not a baby!"

"Oh, honey," Ms. Baldwin said sadly, her eyes all soggy-looking. "Were you listening?"

Izzy ignored the question. "Oliver's going to be fine, isn't he, Mom? His life isn't *ruined*."

Her mother reached for her hand. "It's going to take him a while to feel better, Izzy, but over time his pain will diminish, even if it never goes away completely. At the moment Oliver seems better than his father, but I'm afraid he's trying to be a perfect kid for Henderson's benefit. He can't hide his emotions forever, though. He has to feel what he's feeling."

That was the kind of thing her mother always said. You were supposed to "feel your feelings," as if there were any other choice.

Ms. Baldwin nodded her head as if she were some kind of expert on feelings and not just a high-school French teacher. "Sometimes you have to fall all the way to the bottom before you can start to pull yourself up."

"That's not true!" Izzy said. "Oliver's not like his mother. He doesn't have to fall to the bottom of anything!" She quickly went back to pick up her book and then stormed through the screen door into the house. Behind her she heard her mother say quietly, "This has been hard on Izzy too."

Great. Now they'd sit there and discuss *her* problems. Izzy hated the way her mother acted like she understood everything about everybody just because she was a nurse. Well, yak away, ladies. Izzy was not going to listen. Instead she curled into a chair in the parlor where the two boys were busy ignoring each other, Oliver building some kind of Lego fort, and Liam slumped on the couch, staring at his video game again. Yeah, these two were going to be terrific friends.

But as soon as Izzy started reading again, Liam

threw aside his game. "How come your mom killed herself, anyway?" he grumbled at Oliver.

Izzy slammed her book down and glared at Liam. What was this bratty kid going to say next? She glanced at her cousin to see what effect Liam's tossed-off question had on him, but Oliver just shrugged. "I don't know. She was depressed, I guess."

Liam snorted. "You *guess*? Was there a note? My mom said sometimes people leave notes."

"Mind your own business!" Izzy snapped.

But Oliver nodded. "She left a note for my dad."

This was the first Izzy had heard of it. Why hadn't anybody told her these details? A note was very important in a situation like this, wasn't it? It told you *why*.

"Really?" she said. "Have you seen it?"

Oliver continued to press one small, colorful piece onto another. "Yeah. Dad showed it to me."

"Well, where is it? What did it say?" Izzy asked the questions, but Liam sat forward, eager to hear the answers too.

"I don't know where it is now. It said that she loved us and she was sorry."

"That's all? I wish I could see it. I bet Uncle Hen kept it."

Liam snorted again. "If she loved you so much, why'd she kill herself?"

"God, Liam!" Izzy said. "Stop it!"

"I'm just asking the kid a question. If my mother killed herself, I'd want to know why."

Oliver snapped a flag in place on the top of his fort, then sifted through the remaining pieces as if he couldn't hear the two of them arguing.

"He already told you," Izzy said. "She was depressed. You probably don't even know what that means!"

"I know as much about it as you do!" Liam's lip curled up nastily, but then his eyes suddenly cut to the left and the smirk disappeared. He sat up straight and stared at the ghostly presence looming behind Izzy.

Henderson Hook, Izzy's uncle, had wandered into the parlor, tall and slouched in his stocking feet. He looked around the room, blinking his eyes as if he couldn't quite focus them. Oliver stood up but didn't go toward his father.

"Hey, Uncle Hen," Izzy said. "Do you need something?"

"I think I left my coffee cup in here." His voice was barely audible.

Izzy looked around. "Is this it?" She picked up a mug from the table beside her.

Uncle Henderson stared at the mug. "I guess so."

"It's cold," Izzy said. "It's been sitting here all

day." Actually, Izzy thought, it might have been there since the day before.

Finally her uncle's gaze landed on her face. "What time is it?"

"About three o'clock."

"In the afternoon?"

Liam made a strangled sound in his throat.

"Yeah."

"Guess I lost track." The foggy look on her uncle's face scared Izzy. The Uncle Henderson she'd always known—the loud, funny guy who was never without a guitar hanging from his neck—had vanished inside this shadow-man who could barely speak.

"I'll warm it up for you, Dad," Oliver said, approaching his father cautiously. "Do you want me to put it in the microwave?"

"Okay," Uncle Henderson said. "I guess so."

Oliver grabbed the cup from Izzy and almost spilled the leftover coffee as he dashed from the room. His father lumbered slowly after him.

As soon as they were both gone, Liam exploded with laughter. "Oh my God, no wonder the kid's a psycho. His father's crazy too! The guy doesn't know if it's daytime or the middle of the night!"

Izzy looked around for something to throw at the idiot, but the only thing available was a lamp. It was an ugly lamp, but her mother would probably still be mad to have it smashed, even for a good cause. Instead Izzy stood up and made her eyes into thin slits. "You are evil, Liam Baldwin. An evil little creep."

"Takes one to know one," he shot back.

"Get out of here!" she yelled at him. She pulled off one of her ill-fitting sneakers and hurled it across the room. Liam ducked away from it, but she was glad to see a spark of fear in his dark little eyes.

"No problem," he said. "You're *all* crazy."

As he headed for the door, Izzy chased him for just a second, and he ran. He *ran*. And she felt good about that.

CHAPTER
3

After dinner Izzy sat cross-legged on her bed, watching the movie *The Heat* on her computer for the third time. (It was R-rated, but mostly for language, and she'd heard worse from kids at school.) She loved it for the way her favorite comic actresses, Melissa McCarthy and Sandra Bullock, pulled off the humor. Sandra would set up the joke in her deadpan style, and then Melissa would knock it out of the park. No stupid mime could make people laugh like that. If you laughed at a mime, it was because you were glad he was making fun of somebody else and not you.

Before her parents got divorced, Izzy used to watch a lot of comedy with her dad. His favorite comedian was Jerry Seinfeld, but he liked Ellen DeGeneres a lot too. He always said, "I love watching people who can work a crowd like that."

Apparently her dad had once wanted to be a stand-up comedian himself and had gone to a few open-mic nights in New York as a young man. But then he grew up and got kind of boring, like most adults, and his love of comedy became this secret thing he didn't talk about very much, except to Izzy, who was more than happy to listen.

"With Seinfeld, the first line of the joke is funny already," he'd explain. "For example, he starts out, 'What's the deal with war?' You're laughing already because nobody seriously asks a question like that. It's not a real question—it's too *big*. And then the joke is about how the Swiss fight with those little Swiss Army knives—bottle openers and spoons. And then he finishes the routine with the best line of all. 'Back off—I've got the toe clippers!' You see how he builds up to the funniest line?"

Izzy did see. And she loved that her dad thought she was smart enough to understand how the jokes worked. She loved laughing so hard that they'd fall over sideways on the couch, gasping for breath. And she loved the feeling of power she got when *she* said something funny and her dad laughed at *her*.

But that hadn't happened in a long time. It had been two and a half years since her parents had divorced and her dad had moved to Boston. When Izzy visited, he was never in the mood to watch stand-up anymore, or even *Saturday Night Live* or a funny movie. At first he was too sad, then he was too busy, then he was too in love. These days Izzy watched comedy by herself, and sometimes she worked on a routine. She thought about which jokes might make her dad laugh. Or even just make him look at her again.

Izzy climbed off her bed and stood in front of the full-length mirror that hung on her closet door. She was wearing an old pair of pajamas that was too small for her. The legs ended halfway between her ankles and her knees, which made her legs look scrawny and her feet look big. Was it funny? She wasn't sure. Most stand-up comedians had a certain look. They had a stage costume. Jerry always wore suits and ties, Ellen had jeans and sneakers, and Joan Rivers got decked out in jewelry and furs. You had to have an image. Could small pajamas be her look?

She stood so that her feet fanned out sideways, and they looked bigger and sillier.

"So, what's the deal with . . . ," she began, then stopped. The deal with what? She looked around her room. "What's the deal with shoes?" she said to the mirror. "Cavemen didn't wear shoes. Why do we stuff our feet into little leather canoes, anyway?" Nope, wasn't funny. What would Ellen say about shoes? Maybe there wasn't anything funny about shoes.

"So, what's the deal with . . . school?" *That* was a good topic. "The first few years, sure: you learn to read, you count to a hundred, red and blue makes purple—that's good stuff. But after that . . ." She thought about Jerry; how he built the joke and then *sold* it. "After that it's such a hassle! Every day you have to figure out what to wear so you'll be . . . inconspicuous enough not to be called on in class, but . . . not so invisible that nobody sits with you in the cafeteria. You gotta do well enough on the test so your parents don't freak out, but not so good that . . . the teacher wants you to join the math team."

Not bad, she thought. What else?

"Because if you think you're walking that tightrope *now*—you know, the one between 'I can almost see popularity from here' and 'maybe if I shaved my head someone would notice me'—once you become a mathlete . . . once you sign up for *mathletics* . . . , you might as well just go eat lunch with the school librarian, because you've become a complete social misfit."

"Ha!" The burst of laughter startled Izzy.

"The way you tell it is funny," Oliver said. "Mathletics!" He leaned in the doorway, critiquing her performance.

Izzy whirled around. "God, Oliver, how long have you been watching me?"

"Not that long. Also, I don't see what's so bad about eating lunch with the school librarian."

"Who asked you? You were spying on me!"

"Your door was open."

Izzy stomped over to him. "Well, it isn't now!" she said as she swung it closed in his face.

But she could still hear him. "It would be funnier," Oliver shouted, "if you really did shave your head!"

Izzy burned for another moment over being caught, but then she remembered what Oliver had said. "The way you tell it is funny." He'd actually laughed. Oliver, who hardly ever laughed at anything anymore, had laughed at *her* joke.

CHAPTER 4

"I can't believe your mother is dating Dr. Gustino now. That's just so weird," Pauline said as she unrolled her sleeping bag on Izzy's bedroom floor.

It was the first time Pauline and Cookie had spent the night at Izzy's all summer. Cookie was just back from seven weeks at sleepaway camp, which she could not stop talking about, and Pauline had gone to London with her family for an even longer time while her father did research for a new book.

Usually Izzy's mother didn't like her to have

people over while she was out for the evening, but this time she'd suggested it. She'd said, "A few more eyes can't hurt," which Izzy didn't quite understand. Were the girls supposed to be baby-sitting Oliver? Or Uncle Henderson? Or were they all supposed to be watching each other while the one functioning adult was away for a few hours?

"I think Dr. Gustino's kind of cute," Cookie said. "You know, for a dentist." She stood in front of Izzy's mirror, arranging her long hair, sun-bleached after the summer, into graceful waves that fell over her shoulders.

"There's just something about dentists, though," Pauline said, a shudder passing through her body. "They have to put their hands in people's mouths all day long."

Cookie agreed. "It's kind of disgusting."

What's the deal with dentists? Izzy thought, but no hilarious answers came to her. It was hard to concentrate when Cookie and Pauline were talking.

"Plus," Pauline continued, "Dr. Gustino has that awful son. You don't have to hang out with him ever, do you?"

Izzy was not interested in discussing Ben Gustino. She'd caught a glimpse of herself in the mirror behind her friends' heads, and she was thinking about her disappointing hair. It was not long and flowy like Cookie's, nor was it black and spiky like the pixie cut Pauline had returned with from England. No, Izzy's hair was thin and brownish and straggly, and she tended to shove it behind her ears just to get it out of the way. But she'd be starting seventh grade in a few days, and she was tired of looking like her same old boring self. Maybe she should dye her hair a bright color, like some of the high-school girls did. Pink or green or turquoise.

Pauline snapped her fingers in front of Izzy's face. "Where are you? I asked you about Ben Gustino."

"I hardly even know him," Izzy said. "Do you think he's gonna hang around with a seventh grader? He's in high school!"

"You're lucky you don't have to see him," Cookie said. "My brother *hates* him. He's such a bully."

"That's what my sister says too," Pauline said. "She's two years older than he is, and she's *still* scared of him."

"That doesn't prove anything," Izzy said. "Trish is scared of her shadow. What did he do that's so terrible?" Izzy had seen Ben twice when she'd gone with her mother to Dr. Gustino's for dinner, but he'd never eaten with them. He didn't bother with an excuse—he'd just walk out of the house a few minutes after their arrival. Even though she knew

Ben was dissing her and her mother by leaving, there was a part of her that admired him for it. If she'd had the nerve, Izzy would have bailed on those dull dinners too. It hadn't occurred to her that Ben was anything worse than just a normal, rude teenager. *What's the deal with teenagers, anyway?* There must be something funny about them, but Izzy didn't actually know enough about the species to pin down a joke. The only ones she was close enough to observe were her friends' older siblings, and both of them were too dull to be amusing.

"Trish says Ben Gustino beats people up for no reason at all," Pauline said. "You just have to look at him sideways. He's, like, mad all the time."

"Adam told me he got kicked off the baseball team for throwing a bat at somebody's head and giving the kid a concussion," Cookie said.

Great. Just what they needed around here, another person with problems. Not that Izzy was worried about Ben becoming an actual family member. Her mother had dated several different men since her divorce from Izzy's father, but she hadn't gotten serious with any of them. As soon as a man tried to talk about "the future," she called the whole thing off, which was fine with Izzy. Her mother always said, "*You're* my future, not some man." So the likelihood that Ben Gustino would do more than pass quickly through her life was small.

(Her dad, on the other hand, had apparently started the search for a new wife the minute he hit Boston, his car stuffed with clothes on hangers and cardboard boxes full of DVDs.)

When the pizzas arrived, Izzy paid the delivery guy and called to Oliver and her uncle. She ripped the lids off the boxes while Cookie set the table with plates and napkins. Pauline poured apple cider into glasses.

"Will your uncle want cider?" she asked quietly. Both of Izzy's friends spoke in whispers when the subject of her uncle or cousin came up. They knew what had happened, and they'd asked the usual, unanswerable question: *Why?* But after that they didn't seem to know what else to say.

"Don't pour him any," Izzy said. "He'll probably get a beer and take it up to his room."

She was right. Uncle Henderson appeared briefly, his long hair mashed in on one side and standing up on the other in classic bed-head style. He slapped one small slice of mushroom pizza on a plate, stopped at the fridge to pick up a bottle, and wandered back upstairs to his room without acknowledging any of them.

"I've never seen anything so *sad*," Cookie whispered.

Pauline's eyes were wide with amazement, but Oliver had appeared by then, so she didn't say anything. Oliver pulled up a chair and reached for a slice of pepperoni. He sat with one leg bent beneath him in order to comfortably reach the table. Pauline and Cookie smiled at him, and then they all fell into a black hole of silence.

"What movie should we watch tonight?" Izzy finally asked, just to get them talking.

"I don't care," Cookie said, then turned to Oliver. "What movie would *you* like to watch?"

Izzy had not figured on her cousin joining them. He'd probably want to watch something childish, like one of the Lego movies. "I thought we'd watch up in my room," she said. "We can stream it on the computer."

"There's more space down here in the living room, and the TV is bigger," Pauline said. "Unless Oliver wants to watch up in his room. Which room is yours, Oliver?"

Oliver seemed as surprised as Izzy that her friends were being so nice to him. "I have the little bedroom. But sometimes I sleep in my dad's room. To keep him company."

"What a good kid you are!" Pauline said. Then she and Cookie exchanged sad-eyed looks, which Izzy found incredibly aggravating. Did they really think that helped anything? In Izzy's opinion, it probably just made the kid feel worse. She knew it would make *her* feel worse.

But surprisingly, Cookie and Pauline did not seem to be having that effect on Oliver. He actually smiled at Pauline. "We could watch an Indiana Jones movie if you want. *Raiders of the Lost Ark*? I brought it with me."

No, no, no! Izzy had been wanting to watch the new *Ghostbusters* with Melissa McCarthy and Kate McKinnon.

"Great idea, Oliver!" Cookie said. "I haven't watched Indiana Jones in ages."

Pauline and Cookie polished off several slices of pizza while they recounted their favorite scenes from the movie.

"Oh my God, that snake scene is so scary," Pauline said, wriggling in her seat.

"Most of the snakes weren't poisonous," Oliver said.

"Does Indy get bitten by a snake?" Cookie asked. "I can't remember."

Oliver shook his head. "Nah. But one of the crew members really did get bitten by a python while they were making that scene."

"Really!" Cookie and Pauline said together, their eyes wide.

Who cared about the stupid snake scene? Were they going to spend the whole evening hanging out with her cousin? That's all she'd done for the past three weeks! She'd been looking forward to her friends' return so things would get back to normal again, and now Oliver was wrecking that too.

Finally Izzy interrupted the Indiana Jones conversation. "Cookie, you were starting to tell us before about that guy at your camp." Not that Izzy really wanted to hear Cookie brag about some boy who'd probably fallen in love with her hair, but at least it was a subject Oliver wouldn't be interested in. Maybe he'd get bored and leave them alone.

Cookie only hesitated for a second. "Oh my God, you would not believe how cute Tyler is. Wait! I've got a picture!" She pulled her phone from her pocket and tapped around on it. Which was annoying because, of the three of them, Izzy was the only one who didn't yet have her own cell phone. Her mother thought twelve (and a half!) was too young to begin an addiction to electronics. Like a smartphone was marijuana or something.

Cookie handed the phone to Izzy. There was a picture of a kid with brown hair and a big nose. What, Izzy wondered, made this ordinary boy seem so special to her friend? Izzy thought his crooked smile made him look untrustworthy, but she knew what her response was supposed to be. "Cute," she said, and handed the phone to Pauline.

"We got together the fifth week we were there," Cookie said. "At first he was going out with this girl, Amanda, but then one day during free swim at the lake he was sort of flirting with me, and Amanda got mad, so she stopped speaking to him, and to me too, of course, but I didn't care because it was like suddenly *I* was going out with Tyler. I mean, we didn't actually say that, but . . ."

"But what?" Pauline hung on every word that tumbled out of Cookie's mouth.

Cookie glanced at Oliver. "Well, you know. He kissed me."

Pauline sighed. "*Really*? What was it like?"

Izzy wrinkled up her nose. She couldn't help it. The idea of swapping spit with some sweaty boy just didn't appeal to her, and she couldn't imagine it ever would.

"What are you making that face for?" Cookie asked her.

"I don't think we should be talking about kissing in front of Oliver," Izzy said. "He's a little kid."

Oliver kicked her under the table. "I'm only two years younger than you, Izzy. I know about kissing."

"Two and a half," Izzy corrected him. "And I doubt you know very *much* about it."

"I'm not giving him details," Cookie said. "It was just . . . very nice. We kissed a few times. But then I heard he kissed another girl too. Liz Baker."

"Jeez, is that all anybody does at that camp? Kiss everybody?" Izzy decided she was never going to camp, ever.

"No, we did lots of stuff. Swimming and archery and hiking. We put on a play and rode horses. It was a lot more fun than walking around downtown Coolidge all summer or swimming in that muddy river."

"I like the river," Izzy said, though in fact she'd only gone swimming there once all summer. She thought she might actually like to go to a camp where you rode horses, but she knew that ever since her dad had left, there was no extra money for things like that, so there was no point wishing. If she asked about it, she'd probably get the lecture again about how they were a one-income family now, and then her mom would start in on how the house needed a new roof, and did Izzy have any idea how much that cost. No, she didn't. How the heck was she supposed to know about stuff like that?

Pauline was impatient to get back to the subject at hand. "So, did you break up with him? When he kissed that other girl?"

"Well, I was really mad, of course, but he apologized for it. I'm not sure if we're still going together or not. He said he'd email me, but then I heard he told Liz that too."

Just as Izzy suspected: untrustworthy. And yet Cookie didn't seem that upset about it. In fact, telling the story had her so excited, she bounced in her chair.

"Your summer was a lot better than mine," Pauline said.

"Didn't you meet any cute boys in London?" Cookie asked.

"There was one boy who lived in the same building we did, but I was too nervous to talk to him."

"Oh, Pauline!" Cookie said sympathetically.

"Are you kidding?" Izzy said. "You got to spend the whole summer in London, and you're bummed because you didn't talk to some stupid boy? Didn't you walk around the city and see cool stuff? You told me you were going on that big Ferris wheel thing."

"The London Eye. Of course we did, but I was with my parents the whole time. What fun is that?"

More fun than playing Boggle with your nerdy, freaked-out cousin.

"Did you go into Boston this summer, like last year?" Cookie asked Izzy.

"Just for a few days right after school got out," she said. "Dad was pretty busy." She could have stayed longer, but she didn't want to. The summer before, she'd stayed for a month, and it had been awful. She'd hardly spent any time with her father—just that one Saturday when his girlfriend, Emily, was busy with something or other, and Izzy had suggested to her dad that they watch some DVDs of old *Saturday Night Live* shows together. That had been an excellent day, almost like old times. But most of the month, she'd had to hang out with Emily and help her get ready to become Wife Number Two. She'd accompanied the constantly babbling woman to look at flowers and wedding cakes and bridesmaids' dresses, one of which Izzy had been forced to wear for the big event last Christmas.

Izzy was uncomfortable around her father now that he was all lovey-dovey with Emily. It seemed like he'd erased her mother from his memory, as if she'd never existed. And if her mother never existed, where did Izzy fit into the picture? It was as if her dad and Emily—whose last name was now Shepherd too—were riding a tandem bike, and Izzy was dragging along behind them on a tricycle. She couldn't keep up, and after a while she didn't even want to. Izzy hoped that someday, maybe when her stand-up routine was perfected, he'd pay attention to her again.

"I just had a great idea!" Pauline said. "My dad is going into Boston for a meeting at UMass on Friday morning, and he's staying overnight at a hotel. If we went in with him, we could sleep over at your dad's and go school shopping on Newbury Street!"

"Can we, Izzy?" Cookie asked. "I need some

new stuff, and I can never find anything in downtown Coolidge."

Really? They wanted to go all the way to Boston just to shop? Sometimes Izzy hardly recognized Cookie and Pauline as the same girls she'd been giggling with since kindergarten.

"My dad might be busy or something," Izzy said, stalling for time. If they all went in, it would probably be obvious to her friends that her dad didn't care about her anymore. How embarrassing would that be? On the other hand, Izzy had felt Pauline and Cookie pulling away from her even before they left town for the summer. It felt as if they were outgrowing her or something. Like they were getting older while she was still the same little kid she'd always been. If she wanted to keep her friends, she figured she'd have to at least pretend to grow with them. If that meant staying in Boston overnight with her dad and Emily and traipsing in and out of clothing stores, she supposed she could do it.

"Can you call him and ask?" Cookie said. "It would be so much fun!"

Izzy nodded. "Okay. I'll call him tomorrow."

"What should I do while you're gone?" Oliver had been sitting there so quietly, Izzy had almost forgotten about him.

"It's only overnight," she said. God, couldn't

she get away from the kid for *one day* without him trying to make her feel guilty about it?

"Maybe you could come too," Cookie said.

"No!" Izzy hadn't meant to say it so loudly, but *really*? Couldn't she have one day off? "I mean, my dad's place is not that big. And anyway, your dad would miss you," she told Oliver. Actually, she wasn't sure that Uncle Henderson would even notice he was gone.

But Oliver nodded. "That's true. I should stay here with Dad."

Once again Pauline and Cookie pulled long faces.

"Let's watch the movie now," Oliver said.

Since they were being so cruel as to plan to leave him behind for twenty-four hours, there was obviously no question about who was watching what movie with whom. Izzy let them start *Raiders of the Lost Ark* without her while she cleaned up the table. By the time she came into the living room, the three of them were stretched out on the carpet, Oliver nestled snugly between the two girls who'd been Izzy's best friends her whole life.

She plunked herself down right next to Pauline, as close as possible to the huddle of bodies on the floor. Pauline leaned into her gently, a kind of welcome. Nothing else was going to change, if Izzy had anything to say about it.

CHAPTER 5

Pauline sat in the front seat, next to her father, as they headed into Boston, but she stayed turned around, straining against the seat belt, for most of the two-hour drive. "I've got my mom's debit card, but she'll kill me if I go over a hundred and fifty dollars," she said.

"I'll kill you if you go over fifty," Mr. Wong said. "You already have too many clothes."

But they all knew Mr. Wong was just teasing her. He was generous with both his daughters, even if he pretended otherwise. Meanwhile Izzy's mother had given her fifty dollars and made her promise she'd only buy sneakers with the money. "See if you can get your dad to kick in a few bucks too," she'd suggested. But Izzy didn't like asking her father for money. Maybe he'd give her some, but in case he didn't she'd stuffed twenty dollars of birthday money into her purse to beef up her mother's offering.

As the SUV cruised into Back Bay, Izzy felt a headache creeping up her stiff neck and advancing over her skull. The other two girls stared out the window at Beacon Street, where Izzy's father and Emily lived. You could hardly find a prettier street in the city, but to Izzy the stately brownstones—one butting right up against the next, each fronted by a tiny, well-tended yard—seemed dark and claustrophobic.

She wondered if she'd have the nerve to show her dad the comedy routine she'd been working on. Maybe if she had a chance to get him alone, but how likely was that?

You know, they call Boston the home of the bean and the cod, but is that really a selling point? Beans and fish? Personally, I'd rather live in the home of the pizza and the ice cream pie. You couldn't really tell if it was funny until you said it out loud a few times. How would Ellen DeGeneres say it? Maybe it was funnier if you stayed with the idea of a vegetable and a fish. *The home of the eggplant and the tuna fish.* Ugh, no.

"So, what's your stepmother like?" Cookie asked Izzy.

Her *what?* Oh, right. "Emily's okay. She talks a lot."

"She's a high-school teacher, right?"

Izzy nodded. "She teaches drama and directs the plays."

"What does she look like?" Pauline wanted to know.

"I don't know. You'll see. Pretty, I guess. Young."

"How young?"

Izzy sighed. "Ten years younger than my dad. Or maybe twelve—I forget. She was a graduate student when he met her."

Izzy's father had been a teacher at Shelburne College in Coolidge, where her mother worked as a nurse, but after their divorce he'd jumped at the chance to become director of graduate admissions at Emerson College in Boston. And Emily had been one of the students he admitted, in more ways than one.

"I don't think I'm going to find a parking place near your dad's house," Mr. Wong said. "Is it okay if I drop you girls off?"

"That's fine," Izzy said. "Dad said he and Emily would both be home this morning." Which was odd—Friday was a workday for her father, and changing his routine for anything but an emergency was not like him. It made Izzy nervous.

The three girls jumped out of the double-parked car, grabbing duffels and backpacks. They climbed the wide front stairs of the old building, which had been divided into condos. Izzy rang the doorbell for her father's apartment, and they were buzzed inside.

Izzy's friends didn't come into the city often, and they were jumpy with excitement. "I'm definitely living in a city when I grow up," Cookie said. "This is so much cooler than a plain old house in Coolidge."

Izzy didn't agree, but she led them into the elevator and punched the button for the third floor. *Personally, I'm not that in love with beans and fish*, Izzy repeated to herself, practicing saying it the way Ellen would, or Jerry. *Besides, what's the big deal about being the home of a vegetable and a fish?* When the elevator doors opened, her father was waiting for them, Emily peering from behind him. The two of them were grinning that same shaky, unreliable smile Izzy had recognized in Cookie's photo of her camp boyfriend. Yup, something was definitely up.

"Ladies!" her father boomed. "Come right in." He usually at least gave Izzy a quick hug, but today he ushered them all through the door and into the apartment. After giving them a slight bow as if they were a group of visiting dignitaries, he shooed them down the hall to the guest room. Emily walked ahead of them and disappeared around the corner.

"Put your bags in here and meet us in the kitchen," Izzy's father said. "Emily made hot chocolate and muffins to sustain you for your shopping trip."

"Gluten free," Emily called from the kitchen. "I hope that's okay."

They dropped their bags on the floor, and Cookie bent her head toward Izzy. "I forgot how nice your dad is. It was sweet of Emily to make us a snack."

Izzy was on high alert and didn't respond. The three of them walked down the hall and into the airy, remodeled kitchen and climbed onto stools at the counter. Looking out the tall windows, Izzy noticed unhappily that some of the leaves on the magnolia tree in the front yard were beginning to turn yellow.

With her back to them, Emily poured the hot chocolate into three mugs. And then, the minute she turned around with the plate of muffins in her hands, Izzy understood. The answer to the day's puzzle; the reason everything seemed wrong.

So much for telling jokes—there was nothing to laugh about now. Izzy looked up into Emily's eyes, and Emily nodded.

"So, we have some news for you, Izzy," her father said.

"She guessed. Didn't you, Izzy?" Emily said, putting a hand protectively on her swollen belly. Cookie and Pauline took in loud, excited breaths.

"You're having a baby," Izzy said. It wasn't a question. She just wanted to state the fact out loud, to hear what it sounded like.

"We certainly are," her dad said proudly, as if the news hadn't hit Izzy like a punch in the nose. He put an arm around Emily's waist. "Early January. We're starting the new year with a bang!"

"You'll have a baby brother," Emily said. "Isn't that amazing?" She kept rubbing her stomach as if reassuring the baby that everything would be okay, that this so-called sister of his was not actually a hateful creep who'd drop him on his head first chance she got.

"Oh my God!" Cookie said. "That's so cool!"

"Izzy, you always said you didn't like being an only child," Pauline reminded her. "Now you won't be!"

No, Izzy thought, the new baby would be the only child. Izzy would be nothing. She was practically nothing already. Her father almost never came to Coolidge to see her anymore, and when he called, he could never talk for more than a few minutes. Now that he and Emily were going to have their own little family, Izzy would probably never see him again. Maybe this would be the last time.

She bit the inside of her cheek and concentrated on the pain so she wouldn't cry.

Meanwhile, Emily chattered to Cookie and Pauline about how hard it was to find maternity clothes that didn't make her look like a hippo.

What did she expect? thought Izzy. "All pregnant women look fat." The words were out of her mouth before she thought them through.

"Isabelle!" Her father looked at her as though she had horns and a tail.

Emily just laughed. It annoyed Izzy how hard it was to make her mad. "You're right, Izzy. I might as well stop complaining and get used to it. I've got about four months to go, and I'm only going to get bigger."

Izzy chugged the hot chocolate, which was still steamy enough to burn her mouth. "We should get going," she said, jumping down from the stool.

"Wait a minute," Cookie said. "I'm not finished yet."

"You didn't eat your muffin!" Emily said.

Izzy grabbed the blueberry ball and a paper napkin. "I'll eat it while we walk."

"You haven't even congratulated us," her father said. He looked so disappointed, it raised Izzy's spirits a little.

She tried to make her eyes hard and sharp as she stared back at him. "Congratulations," she said. "I hope you like the new kid better."

CHAPTER
6

Izzy led the way over to Newbury Street. She took a bite of the muffin, but it tasted like it was made of fireplace ashes, so she dumped it in the first trash can she came to.

"I can't believe the way you talked to your dad," Cookie said. "I would lose my computer *and* my cell-phone privileges if I acted like that."

"I don't have a cell phone. Remember?" Izzy let her shoulders slump.

"My dad would be so upset if I mouthed off to him that way," Pauline said. She looked on the verge of tears just thinking about it.

"Yeah, well, your parents aren't divorced," Izzy said.

"What does that have to do with it?" Cookie wanted to know.

Izzy didn't answer. They wouldn't understand.

Cookie and Pauline stopped to look in a window where the gold-painted mannequins wore tiny skirts and tight sweaters. Cookie moaned. "Ooh, I love that skirt!"

Izzy followed them inside, where Cookie headed straight for the rack of miniskirts. Izzy wandered toward a wall of richly colored cardigan sweaters. She fiddled with a price tag but didn't really register it. The sweaters were pretty, but she couldn't buy one anyway, and the idea of trying something on just for fun seemed silly.

In a minute Pauline was beside her. "You'd look good in this burnt sienna color. Try one on."

What the heck was burnt sienna? Izzy shrugged. "I'm not in the mood."

Pauline sighed dramatically. "If I just found out I was having a new baby brother, I'd be really excited about it," she said.

"No, you wouldn't."

"Yes, I would! I think you're being really bratty."

It might not have stung so much if *Cookie* had called her a brat, but Pauline almost never said anything mean, so Izzy knew she really meant it. She felt the prickle of tears in the corners of her eyes, but she didn't let them fall. Instead she turned on Pauline and shouted, "Your parents aren't divorced, Pauline! You don't know what you're talking about!"

Cookie came between them, her eyes wide. "What are you guys yelling about?"

Pauline's eyes were brimming with tears. "Sometimes you don't seem like the same person you used to be, Izzy. You're always mad at somebody."

"I'm *not* the same person," Izzy said. But she felt bad about making Pauline cry. "I'm sorry, okay? I'm just freaked out about this whole baby thing."

"Fine," Pauline said. She sneaked her fingers up to her face to swipe at the tears she hadn't been able to rein in, then stomped off toward a rack of scarves.

Under the spell of Newbury Street, Pauline had recovered by the time they got to the next store. "I have to have that!" she said, pointing to a pink fluffy hat with long tails that hung down on either side of the mannequin's cheeks. "Let's go in."

The store carried shoes too, so while her friends tried on hats, Izzy wandered off to look for sneakers. She should have known. This place was too fancy—she'd have to find a regular shoe store

49

somewhere. But, *wait*. Her eyes caught on a pair of ballerina flats that were almost like the ones she'd seen in the store in Coolidge, except this pair was even *better*. Oh my God, they came in silver too! Hesitantly she picked one up and turned it over to find the price sticker. The shoes cost seventy-eight dollars. Izzy almost had enough money, and she was pretty sure that either Cookie or Pauline would lend her the extra eight dollars—they always had cash. Of course, her mother would be furious, but—

"Do you have these in a size seven?" Izzy asked the saleswoman.

"Let me check."

While the woman was in the back room, Pauline and Cookie showed up and agreed to loan her four dollars each to make up the price of the shoes. When the salewoman returned and took the shoes out of the box, they both inhaled loudly.

"I love those," Pauline said.

"Me too," Cookie said. "You have to get them."

She did. She *had* to. Everybody had sneakers, but who else would have shoes like this?

"I'm afraid we're out of the size sevens," the saleswoman said. "But I brought out a six-and-a-half. They run large." She slipped a pair of scratchy nylon socklets onto Izzy's feet and then pushed the flat shoes into place.

"Do they fit?" Cookie asked.

Izzy got up and walked down the aisle between the rows of chairs. The shoes were snug, but shoes always stretched, didn't they? She looked at her feet in the half mirror. She *felt* like a ballerina, as if she might suddenly be able to leap across a stage, graceful and light as air. These were the kind of shoes a girl wore to a dance where she met a prince! Not that Izzy went to dances. And there certainly weren't any princes in the seventh grade, but Izzy was pretty sure these shoes would make going back to school not so bad. They would make *all* these changes not so bad, maybe even new baby brothers.

"I'll take 'em," she said.

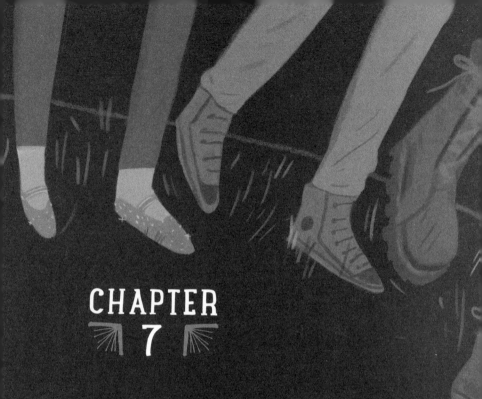

CHAPTER 7

Why had Izzy thought that seventh grade was going to be so much better than sixth? Some of the kids in her class looked about three years older than they had when school let out in June. Boys who'd been shrimps last spring had sprouted long, hairy legs and enormous feet over the summer, and Izzy felt kind of embarrassed just looking at them. But the changes in the girls were even more astronomical. Their shapes had rounded, and they'd traded sweatshirts for tank tops. Their shaggy hairdos had been tamed into actual hair-*styles*. Half a dozen girls wore lipstick or blush or both, and one tripped down the hallway in sandals with heels.

Izzy had worn her beautiful new shoes to school, but everybody had something new and different about them today, and no one had noticed her silver slippers. Plus the left one had started to rub against her heel in the back, and the spot burned more and more with each step she took. By third period a blister was forming, and Izzy limped into history, the only class she had with Pauline and Cookie this year.

Izzy grabbed a seat near the windows and immediately kicked off her shoes. Cookie sat in front of her and Pauline in back. The students were taking advantage of Mrs. Wagner's well-earned reputation for lateness to talk to each other.

"Why'd you take your shoes off?" Pauline asked.

"They're too tight, aren't they?" Cookie said. "My mom always says you should never get the smaller size if they don't have the one you want."

Now Cookie was telling her this? *Now*, after Izzy had spent every cent she had (and some she didn't) on size six-and-a-halfs and made her mother so mad she'd vowed not to get Izzy another pair of shoes this year, not even sneakers, "not even if your toes poke through your old ones!" Izzy suspected her mother might eventually calm down and change her mind, but in the meantime

Izzy would just have to break in the silver shoes. Under no circumstances could she admit to her mother that the purchase had been a mistake.

"Some of the girls got so *big* over the summer," Pauline said, crossing her arms over her small chest.

"What did one boob say to the other boob?" Izzy whispered. "You're my breast friend." Okay, that wasn't original—she'd found it on the internet.

Pauline giggled, but Cookie rolled her eyes. She was a tough audience.

"Why is a push-up bra like a bag of potato chips?" Izzy tried again. "Because when you open it up, it's half empty!"

"Izzy!" Pauline said, blushing, but Izzy got a laugh out of Cookie this time.

"Micah got cute this summer, didn't he?" Pauline whispered.

Cookie shrugged, but her friends knew Cookie had liked Micah for a long time. It had been funny last year, but Izzy had a feeling it was all getting a lot more serious now.

Cookie took her cell phone out of her pocket and looked at the picture of her camp boyfriend. "I got an email from Tyler yesterday."

"What did he say?" Pauline leaned forward.

"No big deal," Cookie said. "We're not a thing anymore."

Pauline's hand flew to her chest as if she'd been hit by an arrow. "How come?"

"We won't see each other again until next summer, if I even go back to camp, so it's silly to be a couple. We should go with other people who live closer to us."

Pauline nodded loyally. "You're right, Cookie. You don't need to get tied down to one guy."

Izzy grimaced. Sometimes she couldn't believe the things that came out of her friends' mouths these days. "God, Cookie, you're twelve years old. Why do you even want a boyfriend?"

Cookie gave Izzy's look of disgust right back to her. "Look around, Izzy. *All* the girls want boyfriends. That's what middle school is *about*."

Was it? Oh God, Izzy hoped not.

"Well, some might want girlfriends, I guess," Pauline said, and Cookie nodded, willing to concede that point.

Just then Mrs. Wagner appeared and rapped on her desk. "Let's settle down."

Cookie and Pauline sat up straight and faced front. But Izzy let her body slump in the seat. They were wrong. Not *all* the girls wanted a boyfriend. Or a girlfriend. *Izzy* certainly didn't want either one. Boyfriends never seemed to last long anyway, and then you felt like a big loser when they dumped you. Izzy didn't intend to be that girl hiding in a bathroom stall boo-hooing over some guy who'd liked her for three days and then decided she wasn't good enough for him. She had better things to do with her time.

°•••••••••°•°

Pauline and Cookie stayed after school to go to the activities fair. They wanted to sign up for drama club and dance committee and a bunch of other stuff that didn't interest Izzy. Besides, she'd promised her mother she'd walk to Hopkins Elementary and pick up Oliver. Not that he couldn't walk home alone. It wasn't that far and he knew the way, but her mother was worried about him starting at a new school.

"He likes you so much, Izzy," her mother had said. "He'll talk to you if he's having any problems."

If he was having problems? Of *course* he was going to have problems. He was a new kid, short for his age, geeky, and to top it off, his mother had just killed herself. His chances of fitting in were zero to none. But Izzy didn't say any of that to her mother. Maybe because there was a part of her that also hoped Oliver would have a good day today; that a group of other short, geeky kids would immediately befriend him, and he would magically turn into a normal, happy fifth grader.

That morning, when she and her mother had dropped Oliver off, Izzy had pointed out the bench where he should sit and wait for her after school, but school had been out for fifteen minutes by the time she got there, and Oliver was not on the bench. This didn't seem like a good omen, but Izzy walked over to the bench anyway, as if her approach might make her cousin suddenly appear.

As she was looking around, Ms. Appleby, her third-grade teacher, came down the front steps and waved to her. Izzy ran over.

"It's nice to see you, Izzy." Ms. Appleby wore the smile Izzy remembered, full and bright, but suddenly it collapsed into a droopy line. "I was so sorry to hear about your poor cousin. I hope he'll be okay here. All the teachers know what happened, and we're going to do our best to help him."

Not another one of those sad faces! She felt like saying, "He won't be okay if you act like the world just ended. Treat him like any other kid." But Izzy knew nobody would. Maybe nobody *ever* would.

"I'm supposed to meet him here to walk home, but I don't see—" But just then she did see him. He was sitting crouched on the ground in a nook between the chain-link fence and the playground slide, his knees pulled up to his chin, his head resting on them.

"Oh, never mind," Izzy said. "There he is." She hoped her voice sounded normal, as if there were no reason to worry about a little boy folding himself up into a tiny bundle underneath the playground equipment.

Ms. Appleby turned to look. "Oh dear. Is he all right?"

Izzy was afraid Ms. Appleby might walk over with her and make a big fuss, which would be the opposite of helpful. "He's fine. He always does that. You should go on home."

Ms. Appleby looked uncertain, but finally she gave Izzy a little smile and walked off toward the parking lot.

Izzy ran to her cousin. "What are you doing back here? I told you to wait on the bench."

Oliver lifted his head and stared at her. His face was as pale and flat as a bleached sheet. As he got to his feet, Izzy reached out to help him, but he shrugged her off irritably. Without a word, he started walking toward the sidewalk, Izzy behind him.

"Did something happen?" Izzy asked as she caught up to him. "Did somebody say something to you?"

"What do you think?" Oliver mumbled.

"Who? What did they say? Is that why you were hiding?"

But Oliver kept walking, silently.

"Just tell me, will you?"

"Why? You can't do anything about it."

"Maybe I can. I could tell somebody . . ."

When Oliver finally spoke, his voice was louder than she'd ever heard it. "Who are you going to tell? My teacher? The principal? Your mom? So they can make a big deal out of it and then I'll be even more of a freak?"

He was right, of course. Once you brought the adults into it, the bullies usually just got worse. It was like poking a wasps' nest with a stick. But there must be something to do.

"Tell me what happened, Oliver. I promise I won't tell any grown-ups."

They were a few blocks away from the school by this time, but still Oliver checked all around them before he spoke. "It was Liam. He told everybody about my mom. He said Dad was crazy too, and so was I, and they should all stay away from me."

"That little jerk!" Why had her mother invited him to their house, anyway?

"He called me Looniver. And then some other kids did too."

Izzy could tell that Oliver was fighting hard not to cry. She laid a hand tentatively on his shoulder, but he shook it off. Well, okay, she wouldn't like that either. You can't give in to it. You can't let the idiots make you cry. She was glad Oliver knew that.

"I'm sorry about . . . what happened to your mom." Somehow the words she'd been careful not to say popped out of Izzy's mouth. She'd been careful not to say any of those dumb, obvious things adults said when people died. *I'm so sorry for your loss.* But she really did mean it. She'd suddenly felt the full and heavy weight that her cousin had to carry around, and she was very sorry about it.

"I know," Oliver mumbled.

"Do you think about her much?"

He stared up at her. "Are you kidding?"

"No."

"I think about her every minute. I never *don't* think about her."

Whoa. Izzy had not expected him to say that. Was that even possible? "Hey," she said, trying to sound upbeat, "tomorrow after school you're going to talk to Cassie, the therapist, right? Maybe you could tell her about Liam and his friends. She might have some ideas about what you could do."

"I'm not telling her *anything*! I don't even want to *go*!" Oliver yelled. Izzy was so surprised by his anger, she stopped walking for a minute, then had to run to catch up.

"Oliver, you should talk to her. She might be able to help you."

"I don't need any help," he said, which was so obviously not true that he snorted after he said it. "Or at least I don't *want* any help. I can help myself."

"Well, sure, but I think you should give Cassie a chance too. I went to see her a couple of times after Mom and Dad got divorced."

Oliver glanced up at her, his eyes narrow with suspicion. "And then you felt better?"

"Sort of. A little." Okay, that was pretty much a lie. At first she'd liked having Cassie to complain to, since she didn't like talking to her mother about the divorce, but Cassie wasn't a miracle worker. She couldn't make Izzy's parents get back together, and she couldn't force Izzy's dad to pay attention to her, so what good was she? Could Cassie have said or done something that would have stopped her dad and Emily from having a baby? Of course not. All Cassie wanted to do was talk about how Izzy *felt* about everything. She felt bad, okay? Really, really *bad*.

"Anyway," Izzy continued, "it's not going to hurt you to talk to her. Anything you tell her, she's not allowed to tell anybody else."

"Not even your mom?"

"Nope. Not even her. That's how therapy works."

Oliver was quiet until they were almost to Izzy's house, and then he said, "How do you know it's not going to hurt me to talk to her? Everything hurts."

For once, Izzy had no answer.

CHAPTER 8

Before Oliver and Izzy had even climbed the porch steps, her mother flew through the front door.

"You're late!"

"Only a few minutes," Izzy said.

"I was worried. After the day I've had, a few minutes seems like an hour. Did school go all right, Oliver?" She lifted his school bag from his shoulders as if that was what was weighing him down.

Oliver nodded, and Izzy held her tongue.

"Thank God for that. Later on I want you to tell

"So, what else happened?" Izzy asked. "Is something wrong?"

Her mother glanced at Oliver. "Well, I came home at noon to see if I could get Henderson to eat some lunch, but he'd . . . well, he'd locked himself in his room and wouldn't answer me when I knocked . . . which worried me a little bit."

"Is he okay?" Oliver didn't wait to hear the answer. He tore the screen door open and raced inside, calling, "Dad? Dad?"

"He's fine, sweetheart! He's sleeping," Izzy's mother called after him. Once he was gone, she admitted to Izzy, "I guess I overreacted to the situation." Her mother's shoulders sagged, and she whispered, "I was so scared, I called Michael."

"Dr. Gustino?" Izzy didn't like calling her dentist by his first name, even if her mother was dating him. He wasn't *her* friend.

"I didn't know who else to call. Michael had just picked Ben up from school—I guess the high school had a half day—and the two of them came right over.

"Ben's a strong guy for his age. While Michael and I were trying to figure out how to get the door open, Ben just went ahead and broke it down. He rammed his shoulder into it, and it came right off the hinges. And there was Henderson, lying in bed, staring at the ceiling. I could tell he'd more or less forgotten there were other people in the world."

Izzy was startled. "Wait. Ben Gustino broke down one of our bedroom doors?"

"I know it sounds ridiculous, but I was so scared when Hen didn't answer me."

Izzy knew what her mother had been afraid of. Was Oliver afraid of that too? Surely Uncle Henderson wasn't depressed enough to do the same thing Aunt Felicia had done, was he? Izzy wished she could shake her uncle and tell him to come back to life and take care of his kid, who was turning into a big screwed-up mess now. But kids couldn't tell grown-ups stuff like that.

"Anyway," her mother said, "I'm so glad Oliver's day went well. At least I don't have that to worry about on top of everything else."

Izzy nodded.

"Sit on the swing with me," her mother said, walking back up onto the porch. "I need to unwind for a few minutes."

Izzy plopped onto the swing next to her mother, happy to hang out with her for a change. She'd loved swinging like this, just the two of them, when she was little. But the last few years, her mother always seemed too busy to do anything so slow and lazy.

"Aren't you going back to work this afternoon?" Izzy asked her.

Her mother sighed and put an arm around her shoulders, giving her a little hug. Izzy was especially grateful for it because her mother had hardly said one nice word to her since she'd come home from Boston with the silver shoes three days ago.

"Nancy is covering for me this afternoon. I'm glad we have enough room for Henderson and Oliver to stay with us, but being the caretaker for both of them is harder than I thought it would be. I'm wiped out. And I have to come up with a decent dinner for company tonight too." She toed the floor, and the swing glided back and forth.

"Who's coming for dinner?"

"Michael and Ben. I wanted to thank them for their help. Really, it was above and beyond for them to race right over here. I told them to come back at six, and I'd feed them."

"Ben too? I thought he hated us."

"Why would you think that?"

"Because he leaves every time we show up. And besides, he's kind of awful. Cookie's brother and Pauline's sister both know him, and they said he's scary mean."

"Oh, honey." Her mother leaned her head against Izzy's. "Ben's not a bad kid. I know Michael has had some problems with him. He's angry that his mother moved so far away after the divorce. I don't think he's seen her in several years. Any child would act out in a situation like that."

How is that so different from *my* situation?

Izzy thought. Sure, she could visit her dad once in a while, but he didn't even act like her father anymore, which was probably going to get even worse after the stupid baby was born. Would her mother think it was no big deal if she started throwing baseball bats at people's heads, like Ben apparently had?

And something else didn't seem quite right about all this. "How come Dr. Gustino had to pick Ben up after school? Can't he walk home?"

Her mother grimaced. "I guess Ben's grounded. Michael has been picking him up to make sure he goes straight home after school."

"What did he do?"

"Izzy, even if I knew, I wouldn't tell you. That's between Ben and Michael."

"So tonight he's grounded at our dinner table," Izzy grumbled. With haunted Uncle Henderson and miserable Oliver. What next?

"It's nothing for you to worry about," her mother said. She gave her a final squeeze and removed her arm. "I'm looking forward to getting to know Ben a little better."

Well, Izzy wasn't, but obviously she didn't have any choice in the matter.

º•••••••••••º

She'd just taken a bag of vegetable scraps out to the compost bin when a car stopped in front of the house. Dr. Gustino got out first and waved to Izzy. She smiled at him but didn't go over. Her eyes were glued to the open passenger-side door, out of which a broad-shouldered teenager slowly appeared. He had black tattoos running up one arm, and there was a scowl on his face. As he walked slowly and deliberately around the car, Izzy could see his shoulder muscles rolling under his T-shirt. Like a lion, she thought. He thinks he's in charge.

Izzy's mother came down the front steps and gave Dr. Gustino a hug, but no kiss. Izzy figured she would have kissed him if both their kids weren't right there. Ben stood a few yards away, glaring at his father.

"Izzy!" her mother called. "Come over here a minute."

Ugh. Izzy dragged her feet as she approached.

"You know Michael," she said. "And his son, Ben."

Dr. Gustino gave her a big grin that showed off his perfect white teeth. Izzy dared a quick glance at Ben, who looked kind of like his dad except more bulked up. They both had thick, dark hair that was almost black, but Dr. Gustino's was clipped and tamed, whereas Ben's hung down onto his neck and fell over his forehead like a horse's mane. But the thing that really made the father and son look alike was their eyes. Their eyes were so *sharp*, Izzy thought. As if they were looking at you with razor blades.

Not that Ben was looking at Izzy anymore. He was busy looking at their house, inspecting the downspout that was broken off halfway to the ground, the porch steps that sagged on one end, the crooked screen door with the missing hinge. Suddenly Izzy saw the house through Ben's eyes. It was an ugly old monstrosity in need of a good carpenter and a coat of paint.

"Come on in," her mother said. "I didn't have time to prepare anything elaborate, but I made a big salad, and I've got water on for pasta."

"Sounds great to me," Dr. Gustino said. "Better than our usual fare, huh, Ben?"

Ben grunted, and the four of them trooped inside.

Dr. Gustino followed Izzy's mom to the kitchen, but Ben wandered around the parlor and the living room, examining everything as if the place were a crime scene. Izzy watched him from a distance as he picked things up and turned them over. The little wooden clock that hadn't worked in ages. The elephant statue with the chipped ear. Was he looking for price tags? Maybe he was thinking about stealing something. Or probably he was just a snoop.

When Ben noticed her watching him, he made a quick movement as if he might come after her, and she jumped back a foot. He snort-laughed, which made her feel stupid.

When dinner was ready, Oliver led his father downstairs by the hand, both of them looking as vacant as condemned buildings. Oliver pulled his chair as close to his father's as possible and sat down, keeping his eyes on Ben, who was seated across the table from them. Oliver didn't seem to be frightened of the unexpected guest, just curious.

Ben peered at Uncle Henderson with half-open eyes. "Hey, dude. Sorry about your door. I can fix it sometime if you want."

Izzy's uncle raised his head as if he'd heard the sounds but wasn't sure where they came from. Finally he nodded at Ben and said, "Oh, sure." Kind of an all-purpose answer, Izzy thought, when you weren't listening to what people were saying. Ben went back to forking up his dinner.

Izzy picked at her food, furious with herself for letting Ben frighten her earlier, for acting like a scaredy-cat in her own house. Just because the kid had a bunch of weird-looking creatures drawn on his arm didn't mean he was dangerous. She had let herself get psyched out because of what Cookie and Pauline had said. Just because Pauline's sister was afraid of Ben didn't mean anything—Trish was scared of everything. The girls had once put a rubber mouse on Trish's pillow, and she'd screamed so long and so loud that the neighbors had called 911.

At first it seemed like nobody but Izzy's mom and Dr. Gustino were going to speak, but suddenly Oliver piped up. "Is that a tattoo of a bug, or what?" He pointed to the drawing that curved down Ben's forearm.

Ben glanced down as if he'd forgotten what was there. "It's a scorpion."

"Oh, yeah, I see it now. And that's a dog on your neck?" Oliver asked.

"*Wolf.*"

"Is there something else between them, under your shirt sleeve?"

Ben nodded. "A bird."

"Can I see it?"

"Oliver," Izzy's mother interrupted him. "Not while we're eating, honey. Another time."

But Oliver kept staring at Ben. "What do your tattoos *mean*?" he asked as Ben piled a second helping of pasta onto his plate.

Ben grunted. "Don't mean anything."

"Then why'd you get them?" Oliver asked. Izzy wondered the same thing. Ben's whole arm and neck were covered with ink that he couldn't wash off if he decided someday he didn't like having a howling wolf climbing out the neck of his T-shirt or a poisonous stinger decorating the lower half of his arm.

Dr. Gustino had been looking more and more aggravated as Oliver kept asking about the tattoos. Finally he said, "His uncle took him to get them, and I'm not happy about it. Not one bit." He turned to Ben. "You're a minor, for God's sake. You're supposed to have parental consent to do something like that."

"It was Uncle Steve's present to me. He wanted to give me something special for my sixteenth birthday."

"*Special.*" Dr. Gustino sounded disgusted. "Steve took you three different times and told the tattoo guy he was your father. He's got a hell— a heck of a nerve. If I hadn't seen the third one crawling up your neck, God knows how many he'd have let you get."

Izzy's mother put her hand on Dr. Gustino's arm, and Izzy could practically see the guy's blood pressure dropping as he turned to look at her. She gave him a quick wink, which Izzy wished she hadn't noticed, then turned away to try to divert Oliver's attention. "Sweetie, you haven't had any of your salad yet. It has that raspberry dressing you like."

Oliver ate a few leaves of spinach, but his eyes didn't move from Ben's tattoos.

"Did you just want people to look at you, or something?"

Ben put down the serving spoon and stared across the table at Oliver.

"Oliver," Izzy's mother tried again. "Let's not interrogate Ben, okay? Let him eat his dinner."

"Yeah, you're totally right, kid," Ben said. "I did want people to look at me. I was tired of being invisible."

"*Invisible*?" Dr. Gustino laughed, but not like anything was funny. "That'll be the day."

Izzy had to agree with him there. But Oliver nodded. "That makes sense."

Izzy's mother looked alarmed. "You know, Oliver, you're much too young to think about getting—"

"*I* don't want a tattoo!" Oliver's eyes opened wide. "It probably hurts when you get it, doesn't it?"

Ben shrugged. "Sure, it hurts." He turned back to his plate of food, shoveling it in so fast that Izzy thought he couldn't possibly taste it.

"My dad has a tattoo, don't you, Dad?" Oliver said quietly.

Uncle Henderson had been scooting food around on his plate without getting much of it into his mouth. He was making tortellini mountains and cutting roads through them with his utensils. His eyes flitted over his son's face without actually landing there. "What?"

"Your tattoo," Izzy said, pointing to his arm.

"Right." Uncle Henderson sat up a bit straighter. "My tattoo."

"Can I see it?" Ben asked.

For a long minute Uncle Henderson seemed to be thinking over his answer to the question. Then, slowly, he turned back the cuff of his shirt and rolled his right sleeve up to the elbow. On his forearm the words *Be Always Tender* were written in careful, flowing letters.

"Well, that's a dignified tattoo," Dr. Gustino said.

Izzy didn't know how a tattoo could be "dignified." Maybe he just meant he liked it better than Ben's tattoos because it was small and not a dangerous animal.

"But yours means something, doesn't it, Dad?" Oliver asked.

Uncle Henderson nodded and lightly touched the top of his son's head. "You're right about that," he said.

"It's the name of the first song he ever wrote," Izzy announced to the table.

Ben raised his eyebrows. "You write songs?"

"And he plays them on the guitar, and he sings them too," Oliver said proudly. He looked at his father's blank face and amended his statement. "Sometimes he does. He used to."

"Henderson records with Rounder Records,"

Izzy's mother said, looking at her brother with a mixture of pride and sorrow. "He opened for Lucinda Williams on her tour last year."

"I don't know who that is, but it's cool that you're, like, a professional musician," Ben said, slowing his attack on his dinner for the first time. "Maybe I could hear you play sometime."

Uncle Henderson stared at his plate and mumbled, "Yeah, I can't . . . I don't think I . . ." Then he pushed his chair back and stood up from the table. "I guess I'm done with that," he said, and walked away, leaving his landscape of food uneaten.

Ben looked confused. "He's done with singing or done with dinner?"

"Dinner," Oliver said.

"Both," Izzy said. Oliver hung his head.

Her mother looked worried as she watched Uncle Henderson disappear, but then she switched gears and turned to Ben. "How was your first day of school, Ben? You're a sophomore this year, right?"

"So they say."

"What classes are you taking?"

"The usual."

"Do you like your teachers?"

"Don't know yet. Probably not."

"Oh, for God's sake, Ben," Dr. Gustino said, "answer Ms. Shepherd's questions."

"I *am* answering them!"

But Izzy's mother was not giving up. "A good friend of mine is an art teacher at the high school. Do you know Mr. Capp?"

"Oh, yeah. Happy Sappy Cappy. What a clown." Izzy had to admit she was impressed with the way that description left her mother openmouthed and silent.

"How do you know Cappy?" Ben continued. "You dating him too?"

"Ben!" Dr. Gustino's fist came down on the table, and the silverware jumped.

But Izzy's mother smiled as if she'd forgiven Ben already. "I'm sure you find it unnerving that your dad's dating someone you don't know very well. It's hard for you to trust me—I get that." God, Izzy thought, was there anything her mother didn't *get*?

Ben shrugged. "Don't sweat it. I probably trust you more than I trust my mother."

"Where *is* your mother?" Oliver asked, his voice urgent.

Ben shoved aside his empty plate. "California somewhere. I don't know. She moves a lot."

"Do you get to visit her?" Oliver's eyes were glued to Ben's face.

"Nah. I don't really want to. Besides, she's always living with some guy. If I went out there, I'd probably just want to kill him."

Dr. Gustino looked like he was about to yell at Ben again, but then his phone started buzzing in his pocket. He glanced at it, then looked again. "I'm sorry," he said. "I better take this. It's my mother." He got up from the table and walked into the parlor.

Izzy wasn't sure if none of them knew what to say next or if they were all being quiet so they could eavesdrop on Dr. Gustino's conversation. Not that she cared what he said to his mother, but his anxious tone of voice immediately grabbed her attention.

"Who is this? This is my mother's phone number," Dr. Gustino said. His words echoed off the walls of the dining room, and everybody put down their forks.

And then he said, "I see. What hospital did they take her to?"

CHAPTER
9

Dr. Gustino looked shaky when he came back into the room. "Apparently my mother had a heart attack this afternoon. That was her neighbor."

Ben's face paled. "She did? Is she okay?"

"She is, for the moment," Dr. Gustino said.

"Oh, Michael! I'm so sorry." Izzy's mother stood up and put a hand on his arm, but Izzy didn't think it had the same magical effect this time.

"She's stable right now—they put in stents, but she may need bypass surgery. And even if she doesn't, she can't really go back home by herself. I need to get to St. Louis as soon as I can to start figuring this all out. This evening, if possible."

"Of course," Izzy's mother said. "What do you need me to do? Shall I get online and look for flights?"

Dr. Gustino kneaded his forehead. "Yes, that would be helpful, Maggie." Izzy's mother got her laptop from the kitchen and set it up between the dirty dishes on the table.

"What else do I need to do? I can't even think." Dr. Gustino seemed to be talking to himself. "I'll have to cancel my appointments for the next few days. I'll call Tracy—she can do that."

"What about me?" Ben asked.

"Right. You can't stay home alone."

"Yes, I can."

"No. You can*not*." Ben and his father stared at each other as if passing secret messages back and forth with their eyes.

"I guess I'll come with you, then," Ben said. "I could help out."

Dr. Gustino shook his head. "No, school has just started, Ben, and this year needs to be better than last. You missed so many classes."

"I can stay with Uncle Steve," Ben said, his face brightening.

"Oh, right. I'm really going to leave you with that idiot. He's been such a fine influence on you in the past."

Ben glowered at his father. "You just don't like him because he fixes cars. What's the difference between putting your hands in an engine and putting your hands in somebody's mouth? You think your job is so much better?"

"My problem with Steve has nothing to do with cars—"

Izzy's mother tried to intervene. "Ben, your father is very stressed right now. Is there a friend you could stay with?"

"I don't trust his friends either!" Dr. Gustino shouted. Then he put a hand on her shoulder. "I'm sorry, Maggie. I didn't mean to yell at you. I know you're trying to help. I'm just at the end of my rope—it's been one crisis on top of another, the past few weeks."

Izzy wondered what the other crises were. The tattoos, probably, and then whatever Ben did to be grounded.

From the far end of the table came a small voice. "He could stay here, couldn't he?" They all turned and stared at Oliver.

What? Izzy had been watching with interest as this family drama played out in front of her eyes, but all of a sudden Oliver had stuck them right in the middle of it. Oh no, that wasn't going to happen. "We don't have any more rooms here, Oliver," she said. "You and your dad got the last ones."

"Wait a minute," her mother said. "That's not a bad idea. There's a futon in the basement, and a bathroom down there too. It wouldn't take long to clean up the space."

Izzy stared at her mother, narrowing her eyes and pursing her lips. *Read my face! Do not let this obnoxious kid stay with us.* But her mother was paying no attention to her.

"Oh, Maggie. That's too much to ask," Dr. Gustino said. "Thank you, but—"

"It's not too much. I've already got a houseful—what's one more? And Oliver likes Ben. I think it would be good for Oliver to have an older boy around."

Maybe if the older boy weren't Ben Gustino! And how about your own daughter, huh, Mom? Is it going to be good for her?

Dr. Gustino looked kind of defeated. "Well, it would only be for a few days. I just have to figure things out back there."

"Is it okay with you, Ben?" Izzy's mother asked.

Ben leaned back as far as possible in the spindly-legged dining-room chair. "Not really, but then, what is? Adults make all the decisions, don't they? Sure, stick me down in the basement."

His father sighed. "Ben, *please*. You have to curb that attitude of yours. Ms. Shepherd is doing us a favor! And if I hear that you've gone to visit Uncle Steve, you'll be grounded when I get back."

"I'm already grounded," Ben mumbled.

"Yes, you are. And if you go see your uncle, you'll be grounded for the rest of your life!"

"Okay, okay. Jeez."

"Can we have ice cream now?" Oliver asked. He looked happier than Izzy had seen him in days.

Her mother winked at him. "Sure we can. Why don't you go get it?"

While her mother booked a ticket on a plane leaving for St. Louis at ten o'clock that night, Dr. Gustino and Ben went to their house to pack suitcases.

Izzy was so woebegone, even ice cream didn't help. Could her life get any worse? Her aunt's suicide. Uncle Henderson walking around in a coma. The Boston baby. The silver slippers that got her into trouble and didn't even fit. And now *Ben Gustino* living in her basement! Maybe Jerry Seinfeld or Melissa McCarthy would be able to see the humor in it, but Izzy certainly couldn't.

She leaned her elbows on the table and rested her chin on her fists. Her mother gave her a tense smile over the top of the computer, and even though her mother didn't say a word, Izzy knew what she was asking of her. *Rise to the occasion, Izzy. Rise to the occasion.*

CHAPTER 10

Izzy vacuumed the old rug her mother had unrolled next to the futon in the basement, while Oliver stretched sheets onto the mattress. The three of them cleaned up the room as much as possible in the forty-five minutes that the Gustinos were gone, and replaced the old, dim bulbs with light you could actually see by, but the space still smelled like a combination of mold and dryer sheets.

As soon as Ben and Dr. Gustino returned, Izzy's mother led everyone down to the basement. Dr. Gustino started sneezing after about thirty seconds.

"Sorry," he said. "I have allergies."

"I know the accommodations aren't princely," Izzy's mother said apologetically, "but I hope you'll be comfortable here, Ben."

Ben shrugged, then glowered at the washing machine in the corner. "I don't have allergies. I can sleep anywhere."

He hadn't brought much, Izzy noticed. A duffel bag, a computer, and a skateboard. He obviously didn't intend to stay long, which was good news.

"So, Ben," Dr. Gustino said, his mouth forming a tired smile, "be a good kid, okay? Be a help to Ms. Shepherd, if you can."

Ben smirked. "You know me, Dad."

"Yes, I do." Dr. Gustino looked sad. Izzy could tell by the way he leaned toward Ben that he thought he ought to hug his son but was scared to actually try it. "I'll tell your grandmother you send your love."

"Okay. Tell her I'm sorry she had, you know, a heart attack." Ben stared at his shoes. "So, aren't you in a big hurry to get to the airport?"

Dr. Gustino checked his watch. "Right. I should go. Are you sure this is okay, Maggie? I know it's an imposition." He rubbed at his nose to stop another sneeze. Izzy's mother assured him it was fine, then took his arm and pushed him up the stairs in front of her. Oliver followed, and Izzy was close on his heels.

"Hey, you," Ben called after her. "What's your name again?"

Izzy turned to face him. If he was going to live in her basement, she guessed she'd have to speak to him eventually. "Isabelle. But everybody calls me Izzy."

"Dizzy Izzy," he said with a smirk.

This kid sure has a lot of nerve, Izzy thought. She stuck her nose in the air so he knew she wasn't afraid of him. She stared right into those sharp eyes. "What did you do to get grounded?"

Ben picked up the pillow Izzy's mom had just put a clean pillowcase on. He squeezed it into a ball and held it against his chest. "None of your business. You tell *me* something. How come your uncle and your cousin are staying here? I mean, I know there's something wrong with that guitar-playing dude. At first I thought he was just a stoner, but now I think it's worse than that. I mean, your mom wouldn't ask me to break down the door just because the guy was smoking weed."

"Wow, you're a genius," Izzy said.

Ben chuckled. "You're kind of a smart aleck yourself, aren't you?"

Izzy guessed Ben was going to find out the whole story soon enough, since he was living here. She might as well be the one to tell him and to lay down some rules too. Just because he had a bad reputation didn't mean Ben could get away with acting like a jerk in their house.

"They're staying here because my aunt Felicia killed herself this summer, and now Uncle Henderson hardly talks or even gets out of bed anymore, and *somebody* has to look after Oliver."

"Whoa, the kid's mother killed herself?" He whistled. "That's major."

Izzy forged on while she was feeling courageous. "If you make fun of Oliver or hurt him or anything, I'll hurt you back. I don't know how, because you're obviously bigger than me, but I'll figure out a way. So don't do it." Her heart was banging around in her chest like it was looking for an escape hatch, but she was glad she'd told him.

Ben stared at her, his eyes filling with anger. Finally he said, "What do you think I am? A monster?"

Izzy yanked on a strand of her hair. "No. But I heard you were kind of . . . mean."

A growly laugh bubbled out of Ben. "Oh, you heard that, did you? I guess I'm famous."

Now that she'd delivered her warning, Izzy was eager to leave. She took a few steps up the stairs and then said, "I don't think scaring people is anything to be proud of."

"Don't you?" One corner of his lip lifted as Ben snarled at her. "Why should I give a damn what you think, *Dizzy*? Get out so I can have some privacy down here in my dungeon."

"It's not a dungeon. It's a perfectly good basement, and you should be thanking us for letting you stay here!"

"Oh, *thank* you, Your Highness," Ben said, his eyes glittering, "for letting me stay in this moldy *coffin*. Now leave me alone immediately, or I'll *bite* you!"

Izzy tried to return his stare, but his anger sliced her like a knife. She shivered, then bolted up the stairs two at a time.

CHAPTER 11

"**I can give you a ride to school,**" Izzy's mother called after Ben. But he was already out the door, skateboard in hand.

"I'm good," he called back.

"You'll be here for dinner, won't you?" she asked. He probably heard her, but he didn't answer.

Izzy and Oliver sat at the kitchen table, slowly spooning up cereal. Izzy was so tired, she was pretty sure the pain from the blister on the back of her heel was the only thing keeping her awake. "I thought Ben was grounded," she said. "Doesn't that mean he has to come right home after school?"

Her mother's eyes were drooping too, but she shook off her sleepiness. "Michael doesn't expect me to police him. Normal life is suspended for the next few days. We all have more important things to worry about than Ben breaking curfew or some other minor crime."

Izzy couldn't believe her mother wasn't taking Ben's sentence more seriously. "How do you know it was minor? Do you even know what he did?"

"I don't care what he did."

"I do. Maybe he stole something or hurt somebody."

"Michael would have told me if it was anything that serious," her mother said. "Don't look for trouble where there isn't any, sweetheart. I thought Ben seemed to be in a good mood this morning."

"Yeah," Oliver piped up. "He high-fived me when he came upstairs."

"He must not have been awake all night like the rest of us," Izzy grumbled. "I should have taken the basement and given him my room."

"Oh, Izzy. One night of interrupted sleep won't hurt you." Her mother was, however, already on her third cup of coffee, and her eyeballs were threaded with jagged red lines.

"I thought it was kind of nice to hear Dad singing again," Oliver said. "I guess talking about the tattoo reminded him."

"I was glad to hear him too, Oliver," Izzy's mother said. "Now if we can just get him to branch out from that one song."

"Yeah, and get him to play in the daytime instead of the middle of the night," Izzy added.

When her uncle had first started playing and singing, probably around midnight, Izzy had been kind of excited too and had made herself wake up to listen. He had been singing "Be Always Tender," which used to be one of Izzy's favorites. But now, when she listened closely to the words, they seemed a little spooky. She knew Uncle Henderson had written it for Aunt Felicia when they first met, but after what had happened, the words took on new meaning.

> *She's a footprint in the sand*
> *that disappears beneath a wave;*
> *a leaf that in a breeze*
> *lets go the branch.*

At first, Uncle Hen's voice had been kind of creaky, as if he hadn't been using it much. Which he hadn't. But after a minute or two, he had started to sound more like Izzy remembered, only sadder.

> *She can't be stopped,*
> *she can't be saved;*

she wants to wander,
wander farther.
She wants to wave a fond good-bye
over her shoulder.

Izzy used to like that stanza. She'd pictured her aunt flirtatiously walking away from Uncle Henderson, daring him to follow her. But Izzy certainly didn't want him to follow Aunt Felicia now. Last night, she'd sat up in bed and leaned forward to hear the refrain and the end of the song, the part she liked best.

She calls to me,
"Be always tender,
a little fragile.
It's not a weakness
if your heart breaks
just a little."

I grab her hand to keep her close,
but what she feels is a demand.
She says, "I can only love you
if you're tender."

She can't be stopped,
she can't be saved;
she wants to wander

wander farther.
I kiss her cheek; I lay my hands
upon her shoulders.

I call to her,
"Be always tender,
a little fragile.
It's not a weakness
if your heart breaks
just a little."

Her uncle had repeated the last stanza several times, the way he did on his CD, getting quieter each time. Then he'd paused for a few seconds and started the song over again. And again. And again. And again. Until Izzy didn't think she could take it anymore. It was a sad song to begin with—the good-bye wave and the breaking heart—but when you knew that the person it was written for had killed herself, it was just about unbearable. How could Oliver stand it?

Oliver had seemed okay at breakfast, but as soon as they got into her mother's car, Izzy could see him wilt. He let his head fall against the glass of the back-seat window and stared out with glazed-over eyes.

Izzy's mother pulled the car into the circular driveway at Hopkins Elementary. "Don't forget,

Oliver, I'm picking you up after school today so we can go see Cassie Clayton," she said. "I think you'll like her."

Oliver made no move to get out of the car. In fact, it seemed to Izzy as if he'd melted into the leather of the back seat.

Her mother turned to look at him. "Is something wrong, honey?"

He shook his head, then slowly leaned on the door handle. Watching him move his arm, you'd have thought it was made of lead. The back door opened, and he slid out.

"Good luck today!" Izzy yelled after him, but Oliver didn't look back. They watched him trudge toward the front steps of the school.

"I hope he's all right," Izzy's mother said. "With all the excitement last night, I didn't have time to talk to him about his first day, but he said school went fine, didn't he?"

"Yup, that's what he told me." I am an excellent liar, Izzy thought.

Her mother sighed and pulled the car back out onto the street. "It can't be easy for him. I wish I could get Henderson to see a therapist. Oliver really needs his father right now, and Hen can barely get out of bed."

"Don't worry. I'm watching out for the kid," Izzy said. Was she? What could she do about Liam?

"Sweetheart, I don't want this to fall on your shoulders," her mother said. "It's not your responsibility."

"I know," Izzy said. "But Oliver's lucky he's got a cousin who's had problems in her own life. If anybody can get him through this, it's me."

Her mother took one hand off the wheel to ruffle Izzy's hair, which was *not* the kind of thing you did to a seventh grader.

CHAPTER 12

Cookie lived close enough to the school for them to walk to her house, but Cookie's mother picked them up because she was nervous about girls walking around town alone.

"You aren't alone if we're with you," Pauline pointed out. They sat on Cookie's bed with a platter of homemade cupcakes between them. A pitcher of lemonade sat nearby on the bedside table. Cookie's mother didn't have a job other than housewife and mother, but she worked so hard at those two that Izzy felt bad she couldn't get promoted to something more fun.

"Plus there are tons of kids walking around right after school gets out," Izzy said, even though she was secretly glad that Cookie's mother had given them a ride. She'd put a Band-Aid on her left heel this morning, but by noon the right shoe had started to rub too, and she was tired of limping everywhere.

"I think that's what she's worried about," Cookie said. "Some of those older kids can be mean."

Izzy had been avoiding telling her friends about the newest visitor at her house, but they were going to find out sooner or later. "Speaking of older kids," she said, "Ben Gustino is staying at our house for a few days."

Cookie's jaw dropped in exaggerated horror. "What? *Why?*"

A cry escaped Pauline's lips. "No!"

"Yeah. They were at our house for dinner last night, and his dad got a call that Ben's grandmother had a heart attack, so Dr. Gustino had to go to St. Louis right away. It was Oliver's dumb idea for Ben to stay with us while his dad's gone."

"Oliver's idea?"

Izzy shrugged. "I think he kind of likes Ben. He was interested in his tattoos."

Cookie shivered. "Well, *he'll* be sorry. I hope that creep doesn't pick on him."

Izzy didn't mention that she'd threatened to beat Ben up if he bothered Oliver. She had a feeling Cookie would find that idea funnier than any of the comedy bits she tried out on her.

"Is he scary?" Pauline asked, chewing a fingernail instead of a cupcake.

"No. Well, a little bit, I guess. He *looks* scary with all those tattoos. And he kind of growls at you when he talks. He doesn't seem to like us much, so maybe he'll just stay down in the basement, where he's sleeping."

"How long will he be there?"

Izzy shrugged. "A few days, I guess."

"God, Izzy, who else is going to move into your house? You barely have room for yourselves anymore!" Cookie said.

"My mom likes taking care of people," Izzy said. "I don't mean like your mother does, Cookie. Mine never remembers to do the laundry, and we eat takeout at least half the time. But she likes to try to fix people. You know, when they're broken."

"Can't she just get a rescue dog?" Pauline said. Her friends giggled, and Izzy smiled with them, but she didn't like making fun of her mother. Even if her fixes weren't always successful, at least she *tried*.

"I hope your mom doesn't decide to have another baby too," Cookie said. "You'd have to move into a tent in the backyard." Pauline laughed hysterically.

Since when was Cookie a comedian? And why did she have to bring up the baby thing? Izzy hadn't even been thinking about it today. Even if her mother *did* marry Dr. Gustino, which was not likely, they wouldn't want to have a baby, would they? If they did, Izzy would lose her mother too. Maybe they'd make her go live with her father. She'd be *lucky* if they let her live in the backyard.

"My mom isn't having any babies," Izzy said. "I think she's too old."

"No, she's not," Cookie said. "Don't you remember last year when Katie Altshuler's mother got pregnant? She was, like, forty-five or something."

"Katie Altshuler's mother is never *not* pregnant," Izzy said. "She's like the old woman who lived in a shoe . . . only she's the middle-aged woman who lives in size ten Uggs."

Izzy thought that was pretty funny for something she just made up on the spot. Pauline gave a subdued giggle, but Cookie just narrowed her eyes like she usually did when Izzy joked, as if she couldn't believe Izzy was making such a fool of herself.

Cookie lit a candle that was inside a jar, and the room started to smell as if they'd been baked in a pie. "I have news too," she said with a sly grin.

She picked up a raggedy teddy bear that lived on her pillow and hugged him close.

Izzy figured this was bound to be another story about some *boy*, and she was not really in the mood for it.

"Tell us!" Pauline could always be counted on to live up to Cookie's expectations.

"I talked to Micah in study hall last period. He sat at my table, and we whispered for the whole forty minutes!"

"What did you talk about?" Pauline asked.

"*Everything*. What we did this summer, and who our teachers are this year, and all kinds of stuff. He's so funny. I could talk to him all day."

"I thought he liked Aviva?" Izzy said. Okay, maybe that wasn't the nicest thing to say, but Cookie hadn't been that nice to her either, saying she might have to sleep in the backyard. Plus Cookie thought Micah was funny, but she never laughed at Izzy's jokes. And really, all Micah did was *talk* to Cookie. She shouldn't get her hopes up.

Cookie glared at her. "Micah and Aviva are just friends. They're not going together or anything."

Pauline pursed her lips and tipped her head sideways. "You know, Izzy, sometimes it seems like you say things just to make us mad."

Us? There was an *us* that didn't include Izzy? She knew she ought to keep her mouth shut . . .

but she didn't. "What do you care, Pauline? Do you have a crush on Micah too?"

Her friends were silent, but they leaned toward each other on the bed until their shoulders touched. The meaning was clear enough. They were a team, and if Izzy kept annoying them, she wouldn't be a part of that team anymore. Maybe she *already* wasn't part of it.

She gave an injured sigh. "Jeez, I'm *sorry*, okay?" But the way she said it meant almost the opposite. It meant *you don't understand me at all*.

"I should go home," Izzy said. "Oliver went to see a therapist after school today, and he was really scared about it, so I need to talk to him. He trusts me more than anybody else." That's what her mother had said, wasn't it? Something like that. She licked the icing from her fingers and slid off the bed.

At the mention of Oliver, the grim looks on her friends' faces transformed into sad masks.

"I feel so bad for him," Cookie said, sighing. "Will you give him a hug from me?"

Oliver didn't even like Izzy to hug him, but she didn't tell Cookie that. "Sure. He likes you guys." It wasn't a lie, but Izzy was aware she'd only said it to make her friends less mad at her.

"We like him too!" Pauline said. "Tell Oliver if he ever wants to talk to us about *anything*—"

Izzy tried to make her eyes look as soft and mushy as her friends' did. "He usually just talks to me. But I'll tell him what you said."

Cookie and Pauline started to giggle again before Izzy even closed the bedroom door, so they missed it when she waved a fond good-bye over her shoulder.

CHAPTER
13

"Izzy said I don't have to tell you about it!" Oliver was standing in a corner of the kitchen, his eyes darting from side to side like a trapped squirrel.

Izzy came in quietly and leaned against the wall, reminding herself not to let her mother see her limp.

"Of course you don't have to tell me, Oliver," her mother said. "It's completely confidential between you and Cassie. I just wondered how it went. Whether you feel comfortable with her. If you think talking to her will be helpful." She had the freezer door open and was rummaging around inside. "Ah, here they are. Do you want an ice pop?"

Oliver looked skeptical, as if she might be offering him the treat in return for his testimony. "I guess so." He took the one she handed him.

"Can I have one too?" Izzy asked. No one had to know she'd already had two cupcakes this afternoon.

"Hi, Izzy." Her mother dug into the box and pulled out another pop for her.

"Let's take them on the front porch, Oliver," Izzy said.

"That's a good idea," her mother said, "but I want to talk to you for a minute first, Izzy. Alone."

Now what?

Oliver ran out of the kitchen while he had a chance.

"Your dad called me this morning." Izzy's mother let that sink in, and then said, "You didn't tell me their big news."

God, was that all anybody was going to want to talk about now? Izzy sighed. "So, they're having a baby. Big deal. He called just to tell you that? I thought he never called you."

"We don't communicate often, but your dad was concerned about your reaction to Emily's pregnancy. He said you were rude to him, and to Emily too. He was pretty sure you were upset."

"Well, I'm not. I mean, I'm *sorry* if they thought that. It just surprised me, is all." Izzy turned her back to her mother and unwrapped the ice pop over the sink.

"Honey, I know this is hard. But I think it's worth starting out on the right foot with the new baby."

Didn't Ellen have a bit about always starting on the right foot? *What's wrong with the left foot? Or was that a different comedian?*

"I know there have been a lot of changes the last few years, and you haven't been very happy with them. Izzy, are you listening to me? Your father wants to work this out with you—"

Izzy whirled around. "Well, then, maybe he should talk to me himself instead of telling you how awful I am!"

Her mother's mouth curved downward. "Nobody said you were awful. And you're right. He should talk to you himself. I'll tell him—"

"I don't want him to talk to me because you *tell* him to!"

Her mother slumped into a kitchen chair. "Izzy, your father isn't always the most . . . What I mean is, he's not good at . . . Oh, I don't know. I obviously couldn't communicate with the man myself, or we wouldn't be divorced. But *you* aren't divorced from him, and I think you need to figure out how to talk to him about this."

Izzy let her ice pop drip into the sink. "They probably just want me to be a babysitter."

"I don't think that's true, Izzy. I think, in the long run, it'll be very nice for you to have a brother."

Why did everybody think that? It wasn't true. She had enough problems already without adding in a brother. "Can I go outside now?" she asked. "This thing is melting all over."

Her mother's smile looked limp, but she nodded. "Go ahead."

Out on the porch, Izzy sat in the swing, figuring Oliver would climb up next to her like he usually did. But he was sitting in a wicker chair and didn't move.

"So, was school any better today?" she asked.

He crunched the ice between his teeth before he answered. "Not really. But at least I was expecting it today."

"Liam again?"

He nodded. "And a few others. Not everybody's mean. The quiet kids sometimes smile at me when they think nobody's looking."

How could she get him to tell her about his therapy? He'd balked at talking to her mother about it, so she'd have to sneak up on the subject.

"Did you walk home after school?"

"*No.*" He said it like she was being really stupid.

"Oh, that's right. Today was the day you went to see Cassie Clayton."

Oliver slurped his ice pop as if licking it was his job. He didn't look at Izzy.

"I liked Cassie when I used to go talk to her," Izzy said, even though that wasn't entirely true. She'd liked Cassie at first, but once she realized that Cassie couldn't help her change things back to the way they used to be, she'd lost interest in the sessions. Besides, talking about her dad moving away had made her miss him *more*, not less. Finally she'd refused to go, and her mother hadn't insisted.

Izzy waited a few minutes for Oliver to tell her what he thought of Cassie, but he just kept working away at the ice pop. She was about ready to give up and go inside, when he spoke again.

"What did you talk about with her when you went?"

"Who? Cassie, you mean?" Izzy tried her best not to sound too delighted.

"Yeah."

"You know, about the divorce and Dad moving away and all."

"Did your dad move to Boston right away?"

Izzy nodded. "At first I didn't mind too much because it seemed better than listening to him and Mom arguing all the time. I figured I'd go to

Boston a lot, and I thought it might be fun to be sort of a city kid. But then that didn't happen. Dad started this whole new life, and it seemed like he didn't want me around much. That's what I was supposed to talk to Cassie about."

"Did she make you feel better about it?"

"Sort of. A little. Well . . . not really."

Oliver had stopped eating his ice pop and was letting it drip on his pants. "So why did you keep going?"

"At first I didn't even know how mad I was at my dad. The more I talked about it, the more I could admit it."

"How does that help you? Just because you know you're mad at him doesn't make you feel any better about it, does it?"

No. Which is why she'd stopped going. Not only did she not feel better, but being so mad at her father made her miserable. It was easier to ignore him, like he ignored her. Still, she didn't want to discourage Oliver, whose situation was even more awful than hers. "Maybe it's not about feeling better. Maybe it's about understanding it better."

"But what if understanding it just makes you feel *worse*?"

"Mom says sometimes you have to feel worse before you can feel better."

Oliver frowned. "Do you feel better now?"

Izzy shifted uncomfortably in the swing. How come they were talking about her instead of him? "Not really . . . but it's possible I quit going to Cassie too soon. Mom said I wasn't finished yet."

"How do you know when you're finished?" Oliver's pants were getting wet and sticky with drips. He stuck the remains of the ice pop in his mouth, crunching it noisily.

She shrugged. "I guess you stop being so mad."

"I don't see why I even have to go, then. I'm not mad at anybody."

"You're sad, though."

Oliver dropped the wooden stick on the porch floor, and his jaw tightened. "I wouldn't be sad if I could go back home to Wilton and be with my regular friends instead of being with all these new kids. In my old school nobody is as mean to me as Liam."

Izzy remembered seeing some of Oliver's friends at Aunt Felicia's funeral in Wilton, a small town in New York. One or two of them had come up and spoken to him in weird, trembly voices, but most of them had just stood next to their parents and looked terrified for the fifteen minutes they were at the funeral home. Izzy was pretty sure Oliver would have had to deal with some stupid behavior from his old friends too, if he'd stuck around Wilton much longer. Izzy knew from experience that when something bad happened to you, your friends got scared, as if they could catch your problems.

They heard the whir of the skateboard before they saw Ben, but it was obvious who was approaching, and Oliver leaped to his feet, clearly relieved to abandon his conversation with Izzy.

Ben jumped off the skateboard at the bottom of the porch steps. He flipped the board up and caught it, then walked up to them, his backpack stuffed full, a long piece of wood under one arm.

"Hey!" Oliver said, grinning. "What's that for?"

"I'm gonna fix your dad's door," Ben said. He leaned the plywood against the porch wall and patted his backpack. "I stopped at home and got some tools."

"You know how to do stuff like that?" Oliver asked.

"Sure. My uncle Steve taught me. He can do anything with his hands."

"Cool!" Oliver looked excited.

"You can't just start hammering around on our house, you know," Izzy said. "You're not a carpenter!"

Ben snorted. "You're kidding, right? This house is falling apart. I couldn't make it look any worse than it already does."

"Can I watch you?" Oliver begged. "Can I help?"

"Sure. Come on." Oliver held the door open while Ben maneuvered the wood, the skateboard, and his backpack inside.

Even though her hands were sticky from the ice pop and she wanted badly to go inside and rinse them off, Izzy stayed on the front porch swing for another half hour, staring gloomily at her too-tight shoes, some of the silver already scuffed off the toes. She didn't want to hear, even accidentally, Oliver idolizing Ben Gustino.

CHAPTER 14

After school the next day, Izzy lay on her bed in front of the fan, watching old *Saturday Night Live* clips on YouTube. How did you get to be as funny as Gilda Radner or Julia Louis-Dreyfus or Tina Fey? Or, in the newer shows, Kate McKinnon and Leslie Jones? Sometimes she practiced a few jokes in front of the mirror, but who was she practicing for? Before long, her dad would be laughing hysterically at some baby who couldn't do anything but roll over.

Later, when she went down the hall to brush her teeth and get ready for bed, Izzy noticed that the doorknob on Uncle Henderson's door was gone. Ben must have removed it when he patched the door and rehung it on the new hinges. As Izzy passed the staircase, she could hear the echo of loud laughter from downstairs.

"Good night, sweetie," her mother called out from her bedroom. She was propped up in bed with her laptop on her knees.

"Who's laughing?" Izzy asked. "That's not Oliver, is it?" Her cousin seldom even smiled these days, much less gave in to the kind of hilarity she was listening to now.

"Ben and Oliver are watching a movie in the basement. Oliver *adores* Ben."

Izzy frowned. "How much longer is Ben going to be here? It's already been two whole days."

"Michael called about an hour ago. He's having a hard time finding a companion to take care of his mother after she leaves the hospital. He's looking at assisted-living facilities now too. I told him not to worry. Ben's doing fine here."

"No, he's not."

"Are you kidding? Oliver thinks he's the best thing since grilled cheese sandwiches. To tell you the truth, I'll be sorry to see Ben leave. He fixed that leaky faucet in the kitchen in ten minutes. It's like having a live-in handyman."

Another burst of laughter shot up from the

lower level. Izzy bit her lip. "Mom, it's almost ten o'clock. Shouldn't Oliver be in bed?"

Her mother's eyes had wandered back to the computer again. "Oh, is it that late? I hate to break up the party. They're having so much fun."

"I'll do it," Izzy said. "It won't be so much fun in the morning when Oliver can't get up for school."

Her mother gave a little chuckle, but nodded. "You're right, honey. Why don't you go down and tell him it's time for bed."

It was so dark in the basement, Izzy could barely see to walk down the stairs. The only light came from Ben's computer screen. As she came closer, she could see the two boys stretched out on the futon, side by side, Oliver convulsed with laughter.

"What are you watching?" Izzy asked.

They hadn't heard her coming, and Oliver jumped. "Jeez, Izzy, you scared me!"

"Sorry. Mom told me to tell you it's time for bed."

"Nooo!" Oliver screeched. "We're watching *Monty Python and the Holy Grail*. It's the funniest movie *ever!*"

"What? You told me last week *Miss Congeniality* was the funniest movie you ever saw."

Oliver looked a little guilty. "I just said that because you like it so much."

"Can't believe you never saw *Monty Python* before, dude." Ben paused the movie. "We can finish it up tomorrow after school."

"Okay." Oliver looked resigned, but then, with a terrible British accent, he said, "I fart in your general direction."

And then both boys recited simultaneously, "Your mother was a hamster and your father smelt of elderberries!" Ben laughed, and Oliver rolled off the side of the futon onto the floor, howling hysterically.

It sounded like a really dumb movie to Izzy, but what boys thought was funny was often a mystery to her.

As Oliver ran up the stairs, he called out, "See you tomorrow, Ben!"

"Good night, Captain Hook!" Ben yelled back.

Izzy watched her cousin go, then looked back at Ben, who'd turned onto his back and was staring up at the pipes in the unfinished ceiling. She pulled on a strand of her hair until it reached the corner of her mouth, where she could suck on it. "I guess you didn't think you'd be here this long, huh?"

"Nothing surprises me," Ben said. "I could've told you it would take my dad forever to figure out what to do in St. Louis. He's not good with the hard stuff."

"Mom says Oliver likes you."

Ben sat up, throwing his long legs over the side of the futon. "I like him too. He's a good kid."

She was quiet a minute, deciding whether or not Ben was the right person to tell. Finally she said, "There are some boys at Oliver's school who are mean to him."

"Yeah, he told me."

"He did?" Izzy tucked the wet strand of hair back behind her ear and tried not to sound wounded. Jeez, the kid had only known Ben for a couple of days and already he was telling him all his secrets!

"Yeah. He wanted to know whether he should spill it to that therapist your mom sent him to. He's afraid she'll call his teacher or something, and that'll make everything worse."

"What did you tell him?"

"Told him for now don't say anything. Wait and see if he can trust her. I've got study hall last period, so I'll skip out early tomorrow and go pick him up. I can put the evil eye on those little fat-heads who're bullying him." He held out his tattooed arm and made his hand into a fist. A muscle in his arm lifted up his T-shirt. "I'll introduce them to my scorpion."

Izzy's eyes widened. "You're gonna beat up little kids?"

Ben shook his head as if astounded by her stupidity. "You think I'm a real creep, don't you?"

"Well, you said—"

"Don't be dumb. I'm just gonna scare the little brats—that's all."

Nobody called Izzy *dumb*. The word buzzed through her brain like an electric current. Her eyes narrowed, and she spat out the question that had been bugging her. "How come you're always fixing things around here? Are you trying to get my mom to like you or something?"

Ben sneered. "Please. I don't care what your mom thinks. I'm bored to death in this place—I gotta do *something*. I guess you'd rather I just hide out down here in the basement all day with my tail between my legs."

"No. I'd rather you *go home*."

"Believe me, so would I. This wasn't my idea." Ben scooted off the futon and pushed past Izzy. He flicked on the overhead light, which was bright enough to make them both blink.

"Don't you have any friends you can hang out with sometimes?" she asked him.

Ben threw his duffel bag on the futon. "I'm kind of between friends at the moment."

Izzy could believe that. "You mean they don't like you anymore?"

Ben had been rummaging through his bag, but he turned to face her. "Listen, Patsy Bratsy, I don't see your friends lined up around the block either."

Izzy could feel her face go red, and it made her even angrier. "I'm just warning you," she said. "My mom doesn't want to get married again. She's not going to be your new mother, if that's what you think."

Ben threw back his head and laughed, but it came out sounding so rough and raw, it must have hurt his throat. "Are you kidding? Having one crappy mother is bad enough. I don't need two."

"My mother's not crappy!"

He smirked. "Yeah, right."

"At least my mother didn't run off to California and leave me!"

Ben glared at her as if he'd like to break her in half. "No, but your dad left, didn't he? Probably because he couldn't stand *you*."

For some reason Izzy hadn't seen that one coming, and the accusation momentarily took her breath away.

"Why don't you disappear, devil child? Isn't it your bedtime too?" Ben turned his back on her.

"I go to bed when I want to!" Which was only true when her mother got distracted, like tonight, and forgot what time it was.

Ben pulled a T-shirt out of his duffel bag and sniffed the armpits. "Well, it's *my* bedtime. So get out of here now."

The lump that had been forming in Izzy's

throat suddenly expanded into a balloon, pushing its way up until it burst out of her mouth. "Just because I'm a little bit younger than you doesn't mean I'm dumb! And I have lots of friends, and I can go visit my dad anytime I want to! And I was helping Oliver too, before you even got here!"

Ben was startled by her outburst. "I didn't say—"

But Izzy didn't stick around to listen. She made for the stairs before the tears she hadn't even realized were gathering spilled down her cheeks.

"And this is my house!" she yelled back at him as she stomped upstairs. "So don't you ever tell me to *get out of here*! You're the one who should get out, and I can't wait until you do!"

CHAPTER 15

Dr. Gustino called Friday night after dinner. He talked to Ben first, though not for long. The only thing Izzy heard Ben say was, "Yeah. Uh-huh. Okay." He sighed deeply, which Izzy took to mean he wasn't leaving their cellar anytime soon. Then Izzy's mom got on the phone and shut herself in her bedroom. Oliver followed Ben down to the base-ment, as usual. Also as usual, Izzy was not invited.

She didn't care. It was the perfect time to carry out her plan. Everybody else—her mother, her father, Aunt Felicia—made big decisions that ended up changing her life, whether she liked it or not. If things were going to change anyway, Izzy decided she'd be in charge of some of those changes.

She'd spent half an hour that afternoon limping around Stuff, the store where all the college kids shopped, deciding what color hair dye to get. At first she thought she wanted Vampire Red or Flamingo Pink, but the Atomic Turquoise looked so pretty when she looked at it up close. Her regular hair was such an in-between color—not blond, not brown, not anything. How could she tell if the dye would look the same on her as it did on the model on the package?

And then she found the jar of Electric Banana. Wow. Izzy hated to admit it, but she'd always sort of wanted blond hair. And this went way beyond regular old blond. It was bright neon yellow. Supposedly it even glowed in the dark. How amazingly cool would it be to have shining golden hair? People would notice her then!

The salesgirl in the store, whose long hair, parted down the middle, was red on one side and green on the other, told her it was easy to do. "Use plastic gloves so you don't stain your hands. Then just follow the directions. You can leave it in longer than they say to. I usually put it in before I go to bed, cover it with a shower cap, and rinse it out in the morning. You get a deeper color that way."

"Thanks," Izzy said. "I'll do that."

"Oh, and rinse it with vinegar afterward too, so the color lasts longer."

On the way home, she'd stopped at the pharmacy to get the plastic gloves, a shower cap, and hair gel, then had run into the grocery store to pick up a bottle of white vinegar.

How hard could it be to cut your hair in one of those punky styles where it stands up all over your head? It didn't all have to be the same length or anything. The first cut was the scariest—her hand shook—but there was no going back after that. As her boring, brownish hair fell into the bathroom sink, Izzy started to feel powerful. Afterward she scooped up the lanky locks and threw them into the wastebasket. Good riddance.

Since the instructions that came with the dye warned that it would stain everything it touched, she got the oldest, thinnest towel to put around her shoulders, arranging it over a T-shirt that was now too tight to wear out of the house. No sense giving her mother any more to be angry about than necessary. Short yellow hair (on top of small silver shoes) would be enough.

She pulled on the plastic gloves. The instructions said to do a test patch first to see how you liked the color, but Izzy wasn't going to bother with that. She'd like it however it turned out—at least it would be different from her usual dull shade.

It would have been better to have somebody else do the back for her, but that wasn't an option, so Izzy just did the best she could. She started slowly, since she couldn't see what she was doing, but then her arms got tired, so she sped up. You were supposed to use the brush that came with the dye, but Izzy just mixed in the cream with her fingers, like shampoo.

Izzy was standing in the shower in case the dye dripped, but the dye didn't just drip; it seemed to fling itself every time she moved her head. By the time she was finished, there was Electric Banana on the tub, the wall tiles, the shower curtain, and all over her bare legs. Finally she wrestled the shower cap over her scalp and peeled off the wet yellow gloves. She hadn't thought ahead about what to do with them, but since the towel was obviously ruined anyway, she just rolled the gloves inside it and left the mess in the bathtub to throw away in the morning.

Her T-shirt was wet, so she couldn't sleep in it. Besides, it would turn her sheets yellow. It was too tight to take off over the shower cap, but since it was ruined anyway, she took the scissors and cut it right down the middle, then threw it into the shower with the rest of the garbage.

Izzy's mother had her own bathroom, so she wouldn't come into this one tonight. Uncle

Henderson and Oliver shared Izzy's bathroom, but Uncle Hen was probably already asleep, and Oliver certainly wasn't going to take a shower on a Friday night. All she had to do was close the shower curtain, then get up early and dispose of the evidence. As she sneaked down the hall to her own room, Izzy felt very clever to have figured the whole thing out on her own.

○ ● ● ● ● ● ● ○ ○ ● ○ ○

It was hard to sleep with the shower cap on, and Izzy woke up late. Fortunately, it appeared no one else had used the shower yet this morning. Izzy pushed the mess in the tub to one side and washed the thick yellow goo out of her hair. The bright color seemed to have stained the tiles and the tub and the shower curtain, but she'd worry about that later. The vinegar rinse came next, but the girl at the store had not told Izzy that massaging half a bottle of vinegar into your scalp made your eyes sting and your nose run.

She grabbed a clean towel as she got out of the shower and patted her head. The mirror was fogged up, so she wiped it with a washcloth, and there, behind the droplets of water, was her new short yellow hair. Very yellow. Neon Electric Banana yellow.

Izzy toweled her hair dry. Hmm. There were a few places she might have cut her hair too short, but the gel would fix it. She wasn't sure how you were supposed to get those punky peaks like the girls in the pictures online, but after some gooey pushing and pulling, she'd come close to the look she wanted. Spiky golden points surrounded her face like a kindergartener's drawing of the sun. She stood in front of the mirror, blinking, so every time she opened her eyes, the full force of the change hit her again. It was amazing. As she headed downstairs, she thought how cool it was that she didn't look like Izzy Shepherd anymore. She looked like a celebrity! Or like a model! Or—

"You look like Big Bird," Ben said the minute she stepped into the kitchen.

Her mother turned around, a cup of coffee in her hand. "Oh my God!" The coffee splashed on the floor before she could set the cup down on the counter. "What did you do to yourself?"

Uncle Henderson, who was busy picking the raisins out of his cereal and eating them one by one, was the only person in the room not staring at her. Izzy could feel her courage evaporating, but she squared her chin and said, "I like it."

Her mother and Oliver approached for a closer look. "Your *hair*," her mom said mournfully. "It was so pretty!"

"No, it wasn't," Izzy said. "It was boring."

Oliver wrinkled up his nose. "What stinks?"

Ben laughed, and Oliver looked pleased that he'd been the cause of it.

"Vinegar," Izzy said. "It makes the color last longer." She was something of an expert on hair dyeing now.

"Oh, now I smell it too," Ben said. "You're like salad dressing on legs."

"The color's not permanent, is it?" her mother asked, putting a finger carefully up to one of the spikes, as if it might be sharp.

"It washes out after a while. Next time I might do red."

Izzy's mother looked as if she might cry. "Honey, if you wanted a haircut, I would have taken you to the salon. The way you cut it, it looks, well, it looks . . ."

"Terrible," Ben said, finishing the sentence.

Izzy was sick of all his insults. "You think you look so fabulous?" she exploded at him. "With your arm full of creepy animals? And those big boots you clump around in? And your pitted-out T-shirts? You're the one who looks terrible!"

She could tell the blow had been a direct hit. The smug look on his face disappeared, and he winced as if she'd hurt his feelings. Who knew he even *had* any?

"Izzy, calm down," her mother said. "No one looks terrible. We can fix this. I'll call my hairdresser and—"

"I'm not going to your stupid hairdresser! I like my hair this way! I like me the way I am!"

As she stormed out of the kitchen, she heard Ben say, "It's a good thing you like yourself, Dizzy. But don't expect anybody else to."

CHAPTER
16

Izzy stayed in her room all morning. Her mother brought her a cinnamon roll as a peace offering, which she accepted because she was starving, but Izzy did not intend to speak to her unless she stopped staring at her hair with that heartbroken look.

At one o'clock Cookie's mother's car pulled up out front, and Izzy streaked out the door and leaped into the back seat.

"Goodness!" Mrs. Daley said. "What did you do to your lovely hair?" Sometimes Izzy hated

Cookie had turned around to stare at her from the front seat. "It's *yellow!*"

"And short!" Pauline said.

"Oh, really?" Izzy said. "I hadn't noticed. What do you think?"

The girls squinted at Izzy, trying to make up their minds.

"Yes or no?" Izzy asked impatiently.

"It's not *too* bad," Pauline said. "The cut is kind of choppy, though."

"It's supposed to be. I did it myself."

"Obviously," Cookie said. "Why didn't you go to a salon?"

"Because I wanted to surprise everybody," Izzy said.

"Well, you did." Cookie shook her head. "Wait until the kids at school see you."

"Why?"

Cookie and Pauline looked at each other and shrugged. "I don't know," Cookie said. "Maybe you should wear a hat Monday."

"Hats aren't allowed in school," Pauline said.

Cookie rolled her eyes. "I *know*. I'm just saying."

What was she just saying? That Izzy should be ashamed of the way she looked? Well, she wasn't.

Later, as they waited in line for movie tickets, Pauline looked around nervously. "Those boys are staring at you," she whispered to Izzy.

Izzy turned to look. The boys seemed to be a few years older. One of them was pointing at her. They weren't laughing, exactly, but they were definitely enjoying her new look.

"See?" Izzy said. "People will notice me now."

"Yeah, but not in a good way." Cookie took a step away from her, as if she didn't want anyone to know they were friends.

"You're wrong!" Izzy said. "I'm definitely pulling off this look."

Cookie sighed and gave her a sad smile. "Izzy, I don't think Lady Gaga could pull off that look."

Izzy fumed silently as they walked inside the dark theater. All through the film, her friends leaned against each other, giggling at the movie, or maybe at her—Izzy wasn't sure. She might as well have been sitting by herself.

Afterward, as they stood on the sidewalk, waiting for Cookie's mother to pick them up, Cookie said, "I've decided about your hair."

"You've decided *what* about my hair?"

"It was a mistake," Cookie said. "You should get your mom to take you to a salon, and they'll get it washed out and even up the cut."

"I don't *want* to get it washed out," Izzy said.

"Well, they'll laugh at you, then," Cookie said.

"Who will?"

"Everybody." Cookie would not meet Izzy's eyes.

Izzy turned to Pauline. "Will you laugh at me?" she asked.

Pauline's mouth drooped at the corners. "You know I won't," she said. "But, Izzy, I don't want people to laugh at *me* either. You know?"

"Why would they laugh at you? I'm the one who has yellow hair!" Izzy tried to act lighthearted, as if she weren't bothered at all by her friends' betrayal, but her voice sounded thin and kind of strangled. She knew exactly what Pauline meant. If you hung around with Big Bird, you must be Snuffleupagus.

Pauline and Cookie exchanged a look that didn't include Izzy. Then nobody said anything else the whole way home.

○ • • • • ∙ ∙ ∙ ∙ ○ ◡ ○ ○

"Izzy Shepherd!" her mother called from the bathroom as she came up the stairs. "Come in here right now!"

Oh *no*! She'd forgotten to clean up the dye mess. Slowly she walked down the hall until she stood in the doorway of the bathroom. Her mother was on her knees, bent over the bathtub, a scrub brush in her hand, the shower curtain spread out on the bottom of the tub.

"Oops," Izzy said.

Her mother's eyes seemed darker than usual, and the look she gave Izzy pierced her skin. "*Oops?* I think this merits more than an oops! I've spent most of my afternoon scrubbing yellow dye off the walls, the floor, and just about every surface in this room."

"I'm sorry. I was going to do it this morning, but then I got so mad when everybody made fun of me, I forgot about it."

Her mother pushed off the tub and stood up, her knees creaking. "Well, feel free to finish the job. I've been at it long enough. I should have made you do the whole thing, but I wanted to try to get the dye off as soon as possible."

Izzy knelt down by the tub. The smell of bleach burned her nostrils, but she pushed the scrub brush over the yellow stains as hard as she could. Her mother slumped onto the closed toilet seat.

"I'm disappointed in you, Izzy," she said. Before Izzy could defend herself, her mother held up her hand like a stop sign. "I understand you're at an age where you need to push boundaries, and dyeing your hair is a fairly harmless way to do it—I'm not mad about that. But you've been acting very selfishly the past few weeks, and that *does* bother me."

"I said I was sorry."

Izzy's mother waved her apology away. "You

wasted my money on those silly shoes when you knew you needed a pair of sneakers for gym class. You act like it's a terrible chore to spend time with your cousin, who needs us so much right now. This morning you were downright mean to Ben, who was only teasing you. And now *this*." She pointed to the bathtub.

"Ben wasn't teasing! He said I looked—"

"I don't want to hear it, Izzy. You aren't the only important person in this household. Uncle Henderson and Oliver, and yes, Ben too—they need our help. We have to put our own feelings aside for the moment and do what needs to be done for *them*—even if it's not convenient. You complain about Ben, but he's been a bigger help with Oliver than you have—and he barely knows him! Ben even helps me around the house. While you were gone this afternoon, he fixed that drainpipe that's been broken for years, and he took the time to explain what he was doing to Oliver too."

"Just because Oliver likes Ben and follows him around—"

But her mother was not ready to let her have her say. "And then I come up here and find that you've wrecked the bathroom you share with two other people—and you haven't even tried to clean it up! I never thought of you as inconsiderate before, Izzy. But if this is what your adolescence is going to be like, we're going to bump heads, and it's going to hurt us both."

Izzy turned back to the stained shower curtain, tears stinging her eyes. Okay, maybe she'd made a mistake about the shoes, and she'd forgotten to clean up the bathtub, but the other charges were unfair. She did help with Oliver—he'd even told her a secret he hadn't told anyone else. Well, he told Ben too. *Ben.* He was the one who was really causing all the trouble. Her mother thought he was some kind of angel, but that was just an act. Underneath, he was as poisonous as that scorpion on his arm.

Izzy had to wipe her tears on the shoulder of her T-shirt in order to see what she was doing. She tried not to sniff too loudly. For several minutes no one said anything.

"Bleach getting to you?" her mom said finally, her voice calmer now.

Izzy nodded, but she didn't speak.

In a much quieter tone, her mother said, "I know this has been a tough time for you, Izzy. There's been a lot going on, and you probably don't understand all of it."

Izzy nodded again, but she kept scrubbing. The yellow stain was not quite as bright anymore.

"We haven't talked much about Aunt Felicia's death, and we probably should. Is there anything you want to ask me?"

Izzy shrugged. "I don't know. Sort of."

Her mother touched her shoulder. "Stop cleaning for a minute and turn around. We need to talk about this."

Izzy let the scrub brush fall into the tub and sat cross-legged on the bath mat, facing her mother, whose hair was coming loose from its messy ponytail and falling around her ears.

"I just don't understand," Izzy said, "how Aunt Felicia could have been so unhappy that she didn't want to live anymore. Why would anybody want to kill themselves?"

"It's hard to understand if you've never been that depressed yourself. It's not the same as being unhappy. It's much, much worse than that. It's a kind of terrible misery that takes over your mind and even your body. Sometimes you can't sleep at night, and then you want to sleep all day. You can't function anymore. You might even hear voices telling you to kill yourself."

"Did Aunt Felicia hear voices?"

"That's what Henderson said."

"Have you ever been depressed like that?" Izzy asked, and for a moment she was afraid to hear the answer.

"No, I never have, not like that," her mother said. "Do you think about, do you imagine . . . Felicia doing it?"

Izzy nodded. "I don't like to, but sometimes I can't help it."

Her mother sighed. "I'm sure Oliver thinks about it too."

Izzy looked into her mother's eyes, which were softer now. "Didn't Aunt Felicia know how much it would hurt Oliver and Uncle Hen?" Izzy asked.

Izzy's mother grimaced. "I guess she thought if she was gone, they wouldn't have to deal with her problems. She didn't believe she'd ever get better." Her mother's hands grasped each other so tightly her knuckles were white. "And I think she felt like she was a burden to her family."

Izzy reached up to twist one of her yellow spikes. She already missed being able to pull her hair into the corner of her mouth. "But they loved her. Didn't she know that?"

"I wish this were easier to explain, Izzy. I have a hard time understanding it too. Felicia had been fired from her job because she was in the hospital so often, and that made her feel like a failure. She thought she wasn't being a good wife or a good mother anymore, and that made her feel even worse. The sickness overwhelmed her. She got into a downward spiral, and she couldn't pull herself out."

Izzy imagined her aunt falling, falling, falling, with no way to stop. "Couldn't anybody help her?"

"Many people tried, but the voices wouldn't go away, and she couldn't stand it anymore. It wasn't anyone's fault." Her mother brushed away a lone tear that dribbled down her cheek. "I just wish I could convince Henderson of that."

That tear amazed Izzy. She couldn't remember when she'd last seen her mother cry. Not when she fought with Izzy's father. Not during the divorce. Maybe never. "Does Uncle Hen think it's his fault?"

Her mother nodded.

"Why?"

"He loved her so much, Izzy. He thinks he should have noticed something that day. But it's not that simple. Hen did everything he could to help Felicia, but sometimes the illness wins anyway." Her mother sighed and gave Izzy a shaky smile.

"At least she's not unhappy anymore," Izzy said.

Her mother was quiet for a minute and then she said, "No, but Henderson and Oliver certainly are."

"Won't they ever feel better?"

"I think they will eventually," her mother said, squaring her jaw. "But it will be hard, and they'll always miss Felicia. Our job now is to keep them safe until they can find some joy in their lives again and start to move forward."

"I think they'll get better," Izzy said, because the other option was too awful to imagine.

Her mother pulled her to her feet and wrapped her arms around Izzy's shoulders. "I think so too, Izzy. I think so too."

CHAPTER
17

Dr. Gustino called every night, but he never seemed to know when he'd be able to leave St. Louis. He hadn't found a caretaker he liked, and he was still visiting assisted-living facilities, some of which had long waiting lists. He apologized to Izzy's mother for leaving his son with her for so long, even though she assured him, loudly, when everyone was listening, that Ben was no problem at all.

Last night Ben had refused to talk to his father, so Izzy's mother took the phone into her room and spoke to him privately. Ben's face clouded over, and he clumped noisily down to the basement.

When Oliver tried to follow him, Ben grunted, "Not tonight," and the younger boy stared unhappily at the closed door.

To prove to her mother that she wasn't selfish, Izzy was determined to take up the slack. She led Oliver to her room and showed him some of her favorite *SNL* clips, but he wasn't very impressed with them.

"Let's watch *Monty Python!*" he begged, until finally Izzy gave in. Grudgingly, she had to admit it was pretty funny when you watched the whole thing.

She didn't really mind hanging out with Oliver these days. Maybe because she was a little bit lonely herself. The first day she'd shown up at school with her neon-yellow hair had been traumatic. Cookie had barely even looked at her, much less spoken to her, and Pauline had only given her pitiful looks from across the room and pathetic little finger waves. Izzy had tried to be angry, but really she was just hurt.

The rest of the student body was even less kind. They snickered at her to her face and laughed out loud the minute her back was turned. The most idiotic of the boys made chicken noises and threw wads of paper at her head.

Today by lunchtime her gelled spikes had fallen over like weeds in a rainstorm. Stubbornly,

Izzy stood in front of the mirror in the girls' bathroom and reapplied the sticky goo, while all around her the cotton-candy blondes and the hair-halfway-down-their-back brunettes rolled their eyes. To keep her spirits up, she tried to imagine what Jerry Seinfeld would say. *Who are these impeccable creatures? You see them at eight in the morning and already the hairdo is flawless—that perfect swoop over the eye, the curl lying on one shoulder. Do you think they sleep standing up? How do they even grow hair that long? Are there horses somewhere walking around without tails?* A little funny, she thought, but not quite enough. It needed more work.

After school Pauline and Cookie went off by themselves without telling her their plans, and Izzy walked to Hopkins Elementary to meet Oliver. At least he wasn't ashamed to be seen with her.

When she got to the school, she looked over at the bench and was surprised to find Oliver talking to a skinny girl with two bushy pigtails. They both looked sweaty, and the girl had a dirty swoosh on her forehead as if she'd wiped a grimy hand across it.

"I'm Suzanne," the girl announced when Izzy came up to the bench. "You're his cousin, aren't you? He told me about your hair."

Oliver looked a little embarrassed. "I didn't say it was *bad*. I just said it was yellow."

Suzanne tilted her head, staring at Izzy's droopy peaks. "I think it's cool. I like people who aren't the same as everybody else."

"That's why she talks to me," Oliver said.

"Oliver told me he was awake all night, listening to his dad play the guitar," Suzanne reported.

"You were?" Izzy asked him. "I had my earplugs in. Why didn't you?" Uncle Henderson had been singing and playing the guitar almost every night, and her mother had gotten them all earplugs so they could get some rest.

Oliver shrugged. "When I sleep, I have bad dreams. Besides, I like to hear my dad's voice. He doesn't talk that much anymore."

It was true. Uncle Henderson's transformation into a ghost was almost complete. During the day, when he wasn't asleep, he stalked silently around the house in white socks that matched his pale face, and at night he just repeated his sad songs. You'd think it would be easy to ignore somebody who never spoke, but Uncle Hen's silence was like that eerie moment before a thunderclap strikes. Izzy kept waiting for a fierce roar to break out of his throat and shake the whole house.

"Sometimes I get tired of listening to my parents talk," Suzanne said. "But if they stopped talking altogether, I wouldn't like it either."

"They keep talking in your head," Oliver said. "But it's not the same."

Izzy wondered how much of Oliver's story this girl knew.

Suzanne pulled on her hair to tighten her pigtails. "Now that your cousin is here, I'll go home. I just live a block that way." She pointed off in the distance behind the school.

"Nice to meet you," Izzy said.

Oliver waved as Suzanne stalked off, her skinny arms and pigtails swinging in opposite directions.

"So," Izzy said, "you've got a girlfriend now."

Oliver made a face. "*No*. She's just a friend. She yells at Liam when he says mean stuff to me."

"Really?"

"Yeah. He's not as scared of her as he is of Ben, though."

"What's Ben done to him?" Izzy asked. A lot of people were scared of Ben for no reason other than his scowling looks. Izzy wasn't anymore, though. He acted as if he might sting you, like the scorpion on his arm, but mostly he only howled like the wolf on his neck.

"Nothing, really," Oliver said, "but one time when Ben picked me up, he said, real loud, so Liam and his friends could hear, 'When you hit somebody, Oliver, go for the nose. It hurts like hell, and it bleeds like crazy.' You should have seen the looks on their faces. That was my best day so far."

Izzy remembered the time *she'd* scared Liam too. That kid was not nearly as brave as he pretended to be.

"Suzanne seems nice," she said. "I'm glad you're making friends. It's getting better here, isn't it?"

He shrugged. "It's okay. I mean, it's not *here* that's so bad. It's . . . you know . . . everything else."

"Your mom, you mean." Izzy didn't usually try to talk to Oliver about his mother. It was too hard to know what to say, so she left it to the grownups. But she couldn't ignore the subject forever. Oliver was a part of her life now, and his mother was always going to be dead. In a month, in a year, in ten years—she was always going to have killed herself. It was something that would never change. If Oliver could deal with it, Izzy guessed she could too.

Oliver nodded.

"What happened when you saw Cassie Clayton yesterday?" She'd forgotten to approach the subject cautiously, but Oliver apparently wasn't as freaked out about it as he'd been the week before.

"It was okay," he said. "I mean, I still don't want to talk about *that*, but we talked about other stuff."

"Like what?"

143

"I told her about Ben. About his tattoos and about how he can fix things. And how his mother lives in California, and he never sees her."

It was as if a gong had been struck in Izzy's head. Suddenly she *got* it. Of *course* that connected Ben and Oliver: neither of them ever saw their mothers. It was possible Ben might see his mother again someday, but still, both of their mothers had chosen to leave them behind. Which was, Izzy had to admit, even worse than having your father live two hours away with his new, pregnant wife. Her sudden realization of what Ben and Oliver shared made Izzy feel a little dazed.

"Did Cassie say anything about you spending so much time with Ben?" she asked.

"She said he's sort of like a big brother to me. I like that idea. I always wanted to have a brother."

"I wanted a sister," Izzy admitted. "I never much liked being an only child." That was one thing all three of them had in common. But of course, pretty soon she *wouldn't* be an only child—she'd have a half-brother who'd steal away the little bit of her father she still pretended was hers. She should have been more careful what she wished for.

Oliver looked at her out of the corner of his eye and said, "I'm not supposed to tell you this, but . . . "

"What?"

"I promised." He wriggled his shoulders, ready to burst with whatever his secret was.

"Just tell me. You know you want to." She didn't really care if he told her or not. How interesting could a ten-year-old's secret be, anyway?

"Don't tell your mom, okay?"

"I won't tell." She crossed her heart with her finger.

"Ben's going to see his uncle Steve after school today. He's *hitchhiking*." The way Oliver said "hitchhiking" made it sound like a felony.

"Really?" This was more interesting than Izzy had expected. "He promised his dad he wouldn't go there."

"Yeah, but he's mad at his dad. I think he's always mad at his dad."

"Where does this Uncle Steve live, anyway?"

"I think he said Eastman. Where's that?" Oliver asked.

"He's hitchhiking to Eastman! That's way up in the hill towns." Even though Izzy would be much too scared to ever hitchhike herself, the idea of it excited her.

"Ben says he hitches there all the time."

"What's so special about this Uncle Steve guy?"

"All I know is he's Ben's mother's brother. And he fixes cars. And he drinks a lot of beer. And sometimes he smokes marijuana."

"Ben told you that? Jeez, if Mom finds out about this—"

Oliver leaped in front of her so she had to stop walking. "You crossed your heart!"

"I know! I won't tell her. I'm just saying if she finds out some other way."

"What would she do?"

"She'd talk his ear off about drugs, for one thing. And she'd tell his father, for sure."

"She won't find out," Oliver said. "Ben's too smart."

Izzy grunted. "Yeah, he's a regular genius. How come you like him so much?"

Oliver thought about it and then stuck a finger in the air. "One, he looks at me. Right in the eyes, like I'm not just a little kid." A second finger went up. "Two, he laughs at a lot of stuff, but he never laughs at me." A third finger leaped to attention. "And three, he doesn't treat me like I'm some kind of a freak."

Izzy digested this report for a minute and then mumbled, "Maybe that's because *he's* a freak."

"Maybe," Oliver agreed. "But he's the kind of freak *I* want to be."

CHAPTER
18

When they got home, Oliver went upstairs to see his dad like he always did, while Izzy went into the kitchen to look for snacks. She hauled out a jar of pickles from the back of the fridge and put them on the kitchen table with a bag of tortilla chips. She was searching through the cabinets for her mother's big pitcher when Oliver came back into the room with a wide-eyed, panicky look on his face.

"What's wrong?"

His mouth was half open, as if he were searching for the right words. "My . . . my dad's not here."

"He must be," Izzy said. "He never goes out. Did you check the bathroom?"

Oliver nodded. "He's not upstairs."

Uncle Henderson had not left their house since he and Oliver had arrived more than a month ago. He hadn't even sat on the front porch or gone into the yard.

"He must be here," Izzy said. "You look in the basement. I'll check the parlor and the backyard."

But Uncle Henderson was not in any of those places. Oliver's eyes were blinking wildly. "Maybe this is a good thing," Izzy said. "Maybe he walked into town for something. To go to the bookstore or the food co-op or something."

But Izzy didn't really think her uncle had done that, and she could tell Oliver wasn't buying it either.

"Let's go look in his room again. Maybe we can find a clue."

The minute they walked into Uncle Henderson's room, Izzy saw the piece of paper on the bed. Oliver probably hadn't noticed it earlier because he was only looking for his father, not an explanation for his disappearance. He saw it now, though, and got to it before she did.

As he read over the paper, Izzy could see the blood drain from his face. He looked like he might throw up or even pass out.

"What is it? Let me see!" Izzy grabbed the sheet from him, but it took her a minute to make sense of the words on the page. What was this? A letter of some kind? And then she realized what she was looking at. It was the note that Aunt Felicia had left for Uncle Henderson before she killed herself.

> *Dear Hen,*
> *Nothing works. No one can help me.*
> *I'm in such a dark place. I love you and*
> *Oliver, but you'll be better off without*
> *me dragging you down. I'm sorry, Hen.*
> *I know you would have saved me if you*
> *could. You were always tender.*
> > *Felicia*

Oliver's legs couldn't hold him up anymore, and he slumped to the floor beside the bed. The empty look in his eyes scared Izzy. Why wasn't her mother here to deal with this?

"Didn't you tell me you saw this note already?" she asked her cousin.

Oliver had to lick his lips and swallow before he could answer. "Once. It was out on Dad's bureau right afterward, but then he put it away somewhere. Why do you think it's out now?"

Izzy had no idea, but she sure didn't like the

fact that Uncle Henderson had been rereading this note and then had suddenly vanished.

"What about your car? Is it still here?" She crashed down the stairs, Oliver close behind her. As they ran across the lawn toward the closed garage door, Izzy was terrified. What if they opened the door and . . . she remembered reading in the paper that some woman in Greenstead had killed herself by turning on her car in a closed-up garage. Uncle Hen wouldn't do that, would he? But maybe it wasn't too late! Maybe he wasn't dead yet. Maybe—

Izzy pushed up the door as quickly as she could, and it clattered across the ceiling of the garage. The car was not running, and Uncle Henderson was not in it.

Her head was pounding, but she didn't want Oliver to know. "Okay, well, the car's here," she said. She was a little breathless, but she tried her best to sound normal. "He couldn't have gone too far."

Oliver scrutinized her face. "You thought he might be in here, didn't you? You think that's what it means, the note on the bed. You think he's going to—"

"No! I mean, I don't know what to think, but I don't think that. The car's here. That's good, right?"

Oliver was quiet for a minute and then he said, "He hitchhikes sometimes."

* 150 *

"He does?" It had never occurred to Izzy that so many people she knew stood by the side of the road with their thumbs out.

"Dad says some of his best songs come to him in buses and other people's cars. He says you meet good people on the road, and even if you don't, you meet yourself. What do you think he means by that?"

Izzy didn't know, but she didn't like the sound of it. "Let's call my mom."

o o o o o o o o o o o

Izzy called, but her mother didn't answer her phone. Izzy left her a message and then sat at the kitchen table, waiting. Oliver was too nervous to sit and kept bouncing around the room. After fifteen minutes, which felt much longer, her mother banged into the house. The three of them did another thorough search before Izzy's mom was convinced that Uncle Henderson was truly not there.

"Well, I'll admit it's odd that he went out by himself, but I don't think there's anything to worry about," Izzy's mom said. "I've been trying to get him to leave the house for weeks."

When her cousin went back up to his father's room to look for more clues, Izzy said to her mother, "Oliver's really scared. Because of the note. He thinks Uncle Hen is going to, you know, do the same thing his mother did."

"It's probably my fault he thinks that," Izzy's mom said, sighing. "It scared him when I had Ben break down the door. I panicked that time, but I know my brother. He would never hurt Oliver. He's grieving, and he's upset, and obsessing over that note probably isn't a *good* thing, but he's also playing his guitar again, which is a positive sign."

"I don't know," Izzy said. "He doesn't talk much anymore. And when he stares at stuff, you can tell he's not really seeing it."

"Henderson isn't Felicia, Izzy. He's upset, but he's not suicidal. He'd never . . . do that. I'm absolutely sure of it."

The thing about mothers, Izzy thought, was that they were always absolutely sure of things. But even mothers didn't *always* get it right. Just because her mother knew how to stitch up a cut or bandage a sprained ankle didn't mean she knew what was going on inside a person's head. And besides, when it came to her own family, Izzy thought her mother sometimes didn't see the most obvious things.

Oliver came running down the stairs. "His guitar's gone too!"

Izzy's mother stooped down and put her arm around his waist. "Well, that's good, isn't it? I think your dad probably just needed some time alone to think things through. I'm glad he's gotten out of the house for a little while, and if he's taken his guitar, I'll bet he's working on a new song. He'll probably be back by dinnertime, and if he's not back, he'll call."

But Uncle Henderson was not back by dinnertime, nor had he called. Izzy's mother tried calling his cell phone, but her call went straight to voice mail. That wasn't surprising—he probably hadn't remembered to charge it all month. The three of them were sitting at the dining-room table— although Izzy's mother was the only one actually putting food in her mouth—when Ben walked in. Izzy was surprised at how glad she was to see him. One disappearance a day was enough.

"Sorry I'm late," Ben said to Izzy's mother without really looking at her. "I went home to pick up a few things, and I guess I fell asleep on the couch."

Izzy raised an eyebrow. *Liar.*

Her mother didn't seem to suspect his excuse wasn't true. "I put your dinner in the microwave to keep it warm," she said.

Ben grabbed the plateful of stir-fry and joined them at the table. "Where's the big guy?" he asked.

Oliver burst into tears.

"Whoa! Dude, what's wrong?"

"My dad's *gone!*" Oliver said between sobs. "We looked everywhere, but we can't find him!"

"Hey, Oliver, we'll find him. Don't worry." Ben got up and got two glasses of water, one for himself and one for Oliver. He put a hand on the younger boy's shoulder. "You're not alone. It's gonna be okay."

Izzy's mother told Ben what they knew, giving him her point of view on the situation and trying to soothe Oliver at the same time. "Sitting around this house day and night wasn't good for Hen. I think it's encouraging that he's gotten out a little. He needed to do that. He took his guitar, so he probably went to visit some of his old musician friends in the area."

Ben didn't voice an opinion, but he looked hard at Oliver. It was pretty obvious that Oliver didn't share his aunt's optimism.

Ben and Izzy cleared the table and stacked the dishwasher in silence, the better to eavesdrop on Izzy's mother's phone calls to people she thought Uncle Henderson might have gone to visit. Oliver didn't pretend to do anything but listen.

The first two calls were dead ends, but the third raised their hopes.

"He *was*?" she said. "Oh, I'm so glad to hear that."

"Where is he?" Oliver interrupted. "Is he okay?" His aunt held out her hand to him while continuing the conversation. "Uh-huh. So you gave him a ride? Oh, good."

When she finally hung up, she told them what she'd learned. "Good news. Henderson went to see Fred Dumont over in Barrington. Fred's a musician too—they used to play together years ago. He says he talked to Hen for quite a while, and he seemed okay."

"Okay" didn't sound all that encouraging, but at least they knew he was alive and speaking to people. Izzy and Oliver peppered her with questions. "How'd he get there?" "Why did he go to see Fred?" "Is he still there?" "When's he coming back?"

"Slow down." Izzy's mom smiled. "He hitchhiked to Fred's house to get a copy of a CD they'd made together years ago. Hen didn't have one anymore, and he wanted to listen to it for inspiration, Fred said. Apparently, a producer at Hen's record label called him a few days ago about putting together another album—isn't that great? He told Fred he wanted to be alone for a while so he could, quote, 'hear music in my head and maybe make some.' Doesn't that sound hopeful? He wants to write songs for a new album!"

"Why can't he write songs here?" Izzy asked.

Oliver had a more important question. "Where is he now?"

"Fred loaned him some money and gave him a ride to the bus station. He said Hen got on the Buffalo bus, so he's probably headed back to Wilton."

"Without *me*?" Oliver looked stunned.

Izzy's mom gave him a worried smile. "He knows you're safe here with us," she said. "I'll bet he wants some time alone to get back to work. I really think this is good, Oliver. Your dad is writing music again. Music has sustained him before, and it will this time too."

"What does that mean, it sustained him before?" Izzy wanted to know.

"When Henderson was young, he dropped out of college and drifted around aimlessly for a while," her mother explained. "He didn't know which way to turn. But then he started to play music and write songs, and that straightened him out."

That was also when he met Aunt Felicia, Izzy thought. Maybe she was what straightened him out.

Oliver's face was twisted with fear. Izzy could tell he was not buying the story her mother was selling.

CHAPTER 19

"Oliver, wanna come downstairs with me?" Ben asked.

Oliver nodded gratefully. Ben was about to close the basement door behind them when Izzy grabbed it.

"Me too," she said. It wasn't a question. She knew what they were going to talk about, and she wasn't going to be left out of it.

Ben glared at her. "I don't think so. It stinks down here. Like my *pitted-out T-shirts*."

Wow, Izzy was surprised at how much that insult had gotten to him. But she wasn't going to be put off. "And you said I looked like Big Bird and smelled like salad dressing."

A smile flickered across Ben's mouth, and he glanced at her head. "Your feathers are a little droopy."

"Ha, ha. Let me in. I want to help Oliver too."

After a few seconds Ben let go of the door, and Izzy followed them down the stairs to Ben's hideout. It was messier than the last time she'd visited. Dirty clothes were piled next to the unmade futon. Soda bottles and half-empty bags of chips lay scattered on the floor.

"I guess you don't mind having mice as roommates," Izzy said, picking up a chip bag and folding down the open end. "If I see one in my room, I'm telling Mom whose fault it is."

"I'm hoping to lure some cockroaches too," Ben said. "I've made them all little maps so they can find your room after I leave."

"If you ever *do* leave. If your dad ever comes back for you."

"Stop it!" Oliver's bark surprised them both. His hands were curled into fists at his sides, as if he were clutching heavy bundles he couldn't put down. "You said you wanted to help me, but all you do is argue with each other!"

Izzy's eyes bounced off Ben, who was giving her a sideways glance too. "Sorry, Oliver," she said.

"Yeah, okay, Captain Hook is right. We need to figure this out," Ben said. He flopped on the futon, opened his computer, and typed something into it. A map came up that showed the route between Barrington, Massachusetts, and Buffalo, New York. Oliver sat on the futon and huddled into Ben's tattooed arm, while Izzy, who didn't want to sit next to Ben, tried to see the screen by looking over their heads.

"So this is where he was," Ben said. "And this is where the bus is going. Where's Wilton? Is it on the way to Buffalo?"

"Not really," Oliver said. He pointed to a spot north of the likely bus route. "It's up around here."

"So, he'd get off the Buffalo bus somewhere and transfer to a local one," Izzy said.

"He'd probably just hitchhike from wherever he got off," Oliver said.

Ben typed "Coolidge" and "Wilton" into the search engine. "This says it's about a six-hour drive to Wilton, which means on a bus, with stops and changes and maybe hitchhiking, it would probably take him most of the day to get there. Or most of the night, if he just left."

"I don't think he's going to Wilton," Oliver said, his forehead knotted. "He wouldn't go home without me."

"Oliver," Izzy said gently, "maybe my mom's right and your dad wants to be alone."

Oliver shook his head. "He wouldn't want to be alone in Wilton, though. That's not where he's going."

Izzy could see his point. How inspirational would it be to go back to the place his wife had died? "Well, where else would he go?" She wondered how this was helping Oliver. Even if they knew for sure where Uncle Hen was, they couldn't follow him.

Oliver stared at the map on Ben's computer screen. Suddenly he brightened. "Move it to the left," he said.

"You mean west?" Ben asked.

"Yeah, west. Way west, almost to Lake Erie. Zoom in on that!"

Ben scrolled the map and zoomed in until they were looking at the area Oliver had requested— the far western corner of New York State, where it bumped into Pennsylvania. There wasn't a whole lot out in that part of the state, no towns whose names Izzy recognized. But Oliver was excited.

"There!" He pointed to a narrow strip of blue on the map. "That's where he's going. I know it!"

"Lake Chautauqua," Ben read.

"Yes! Lake Chautauqua! That's the place!" Oliver was ecstatic.

"Why would he go there?" Izzy asked.

"He loves it there. He used to go there to write songs all the time. We all went once. It's this pretty lake where people go to fish. He's got an old trailer hidden in the woods where nobody bothers him."

"I never heard about that," Izzy said.

"He doesn't tell people, because it's not exactly legal. He doesn't own the land the trailer's on. But it's all woods around there. Nobody cares." Oliver was jumping up and down now. "That's where he's going! I know it! Let's go find him! Then, in case music doesn't save him, we will."

"*Find* him?" Izzy laughed. "All the way across the state of New York? How would we get there? And anyway, you don't know for sure that's where he's going. Even if we could get there, he'd probably come back while we were out trying to find him."

Oliver frowned at her. "You always act like you're not scared of anything, Izzy, so why are you afraid now? If we don't go get him, who will?"

"I'm *not* afraid. I just think we should . . ."

Should what? Wait around here until Uncle Henderson showed up again? *If* he showed up again. Oliver was already coming totally unglued. Izzy was pretty sure if he had to wait for his father to decide to come home, he'd crack up completely.

Excitement sparkled in Ben's eyes. "Come on, Dizzy. Don't you want to have an adventure?"

"But how can we—?"

"Ben'll figure it out!" Oliver yelled. "Won't you, Ben?"

"I'm making a plan as we speak." The two of them high-fived, and Oliver hooted.

Izzy couldn't believe it. They seriously thought they could chase across two states to find her uncle in the woods by some lake. It was impossible. On the other hand, she didn't have a better idea. And she certainly wasn't going to let the kid take off with Ben by himself. "Well, if *you're* going, I am too. Oliver is *my* cousin!"

Oliver clapped his hands. "Yes! But you can't tell Aunt Maggie. You know she won't let us go."

"Are we really doing this?" Izzy whispered to Ben as Oliver danced around the room.

"Yeah, I think we are. Oliver's afraid he's going to lose his dad too, and nobody else is doing anything about it, so, yeah, we're gonna go find the guy and make sure he's okay."

"And bring him back," Oliver said.

"How are we supposed to do this?" The scheme seemed outrageous to Izzy. "First we'd have to sneak out of the house and then take a bus or something. I don't have enough money for that, do you?"

Ben smiled mysteriously. "Leave it to me. You two go upstairs and do your homework, or whatever you normally do in the evening, so Dizzy's mom doesn't get suspicious. Go to bed at your regular time, but don't go to sleep. Pack a backpack with a *few* things." He gave Izzy a look. "A few things. Don't take everything you own. Bring whatever money you've got too. Your mom is always in bed by ten thirty, so meet me outside the back door at eleven and be ready to roll."

"But how—?"

"Trust me, would you?" Ben said. "For once, just trust me."

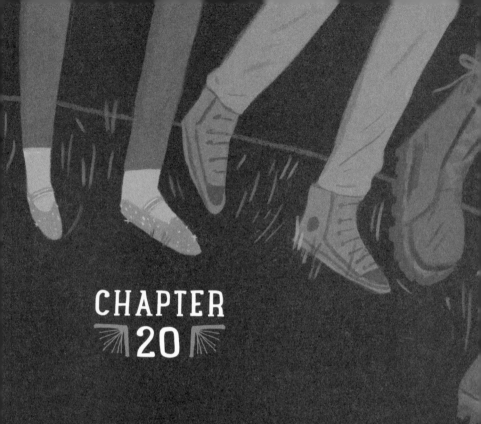

CHAPTER 20

Izzy's hands shook a little as she tucked four dollars into the side pocket of her backpack. She'd spent her birthday twenty on the silver shoes and then had to pay Cookie and Pauline back the money she'd borrowed from them. And all the hair dye stuff was expensive too, so four dollars was all she had left. Unless Ben had a secret stash, she didn't see how they were going to get across the whole state of New York on a couple of bucks.

In fact, she couldn't imagine how this was going to work at all, but she'd told Oliver she'd go with them, and she couldn't chicken out now. He'd been so terrified ever since he realized his dad was missing. She tried to imagine how she'd feel if all of a sudden her mother disappeared. Just the thought of being so alone made her feel sick to her stomach. No wonder her cousin was such a wreck.

Anyway, if Izzy didn't go, Ben would say she'd been afraid, and she wasn't afraid. She was the kind of person who took risks, wasn't she? The silver shoes? The yellow hair? Maybe she didn't go to London like Pauline or kissing camp like Cookie, but her life could be exciting too. And even if they didn't find Uncle Henderson, the trip might be just what Oliver needed. He'd be out of school for a few days and away from those mean kids, and maybe the excitement of going someplace new would help him stop worrying for a little while.

With every item she put into her backpack—a hairbrush, a paperback book, her toothbrush and toothpaste, extra underwear, a T-shirt, and a pair of shorts—Izzy got more excited. She was really doing this!

Of course, her mother would be terribly worried, and Izzy would certainly be punished. Her mother was so mad at her already, she'd probably ground her for the rest of her life. And Izzy would no doubt get a lecture long enough to give her mother a sore throat. But what the heck, Izzy hadn't had any fun in ages. At least if she went with Ben and Oliver, she'd have stories to tell when she got back. If she didn't go, she'd have to listen to *their* stories, and she could just imagine what that would be like. *First this amazing thing happened, and then we met the weirdest person, and he told us the strangest story, and we had the best time, and the whole thing was ten times cooler than anything that's ever happened to you!* No, she was not waiting around here. She *had* to go—there was no other choice.

The more she thought about it, the more excited she became. In the middle of the week, in the middle of the night, she was sneaking off with her cousin and a boy her friends thought was dangerous (who she was pretty sure was only annoying) to take a bus to the middle of nowhere to find some rusty old trailer at the other end of New York State. And maybe they really *would* save Uncle Hen, and when they came back, they'd be heroes, sort of. And Cookie and Pauline would be so amazed she'd done it that they'd forget they were ignoring her, and everybody at school would be shocked by her fearlessness. She could hardly wait to get back!

Still, her stomach flipped over when she thought of her mother walking into her room in the morning. First she'd wonder where Izzy was, and then she'd realize Oliver and Ben weren't in the house either. What would she think? Izzy knew her mother would be scared to death, so she did what she had to do: she left a note. Not much of a note—no big explanation, no clues, just enough information to keep her mother from having a full-on heart attack.

"We've gone to find Uncle Henderson. Don't worry." She put the note on her pillow and looked at it lying there, eight words in black marker where her head should have been. She was going to be in *so much trouble*.

The last thing she did before going downstairs was to try on every pair of shoes on the floor of her closet, but none of them fit her anymore. She'd hoped she could wear her old sneakers, but the sole of the right one was flapping off at the front now, and she couldn't walk in it. (Her gym teacher, Mrs. Tollefson, had told her she had to fix it or get a new pair by next week, but she hadn't gotten around to telling her mother yet. That would not be a good conversation.) Blisters or not, she'd have to wear the silver slippers. She got two large Band-Aids from the cabinet in the bathroom and slapped one on each heel before carefully wedging the shoes onto her feet. The Band-Aids helped. A little.

Oliver was already waiting outside when Izzy sneaked through the back door. He was hopping up and down with excitement and nerves.

"Where's Ben?" he whispered.

"He'll be here," she said. "Do you need to go to the bathroom before we leave?"

"I *did*! I'm not dumb, Izzy!"

"I didn't say you were!"

Ben came through the door so quietly that they didn't hear him until he was on top of them, his backpack bulging.

"You told me I could only bring a few things," Izzy said, "but you brought a ton."

"I brought food. Did you think of that?"

Izzy hadn't, but she didn't admit it. Ben unzipped his pack and handed each of them a water bottle. "You carry these. I'll lug the rest of the stuff."

Oliver tried to see what else was in Ben's pack, but it was too dark out. "What food did you bring?"

"Bread, peanut butter, apples, bananas, and a bag of chips."

Izzy was surprised to hear it was such a balanced selection. She probably would have forgotten the fruit. Well, she hadn't actually thought of bringing any of it.

"I've also got maps, a Swiss Army knife, a flashlight, and my cell phone," Ben said as they left the yard. "The phone's turned off, though— I don't know when I'll be able to recharge it, so it's only for emergencies."

Izzy thought of Jerry's joke about the Swiss

Army knife, but she figured they were all too nervous to listen to it. "What if our parents try to call?"

"I'm sure they will," Ben said, "but if the phone's off, we won't know it. I just hope they don't call the police. I think the cops could trace the phone even if it's off."

Oliver was not happy with that information. "They'll find us, then!"

Ben shook his head. "I don't think they'll call the police. At least not right away. My dad won't want to."

"Why not?" Izzy asked.

"He just *won't*, okay?"

"You're such a know-it-all," she grumbled. "What do we need a flashlight for? We're just going to the bus station, aren't we?"

Ben sighed. "Do you really think there's a bus leaving Coolidge at midnight headed for the western edge of New York State? Or did you think we'd just sit in the station until tomorrow morning when your mother realizes we're gone and puts out an all-points bulletin?"

"Well, I don't know! You're the one who said we'd take the bus!"

"I never said that, Dizzy. You jumped to that conclusion."

"Well, then, how are we going to get there?"

Ben grinned. "How's your thumb working?"

He loped off down the street, Oliver prancing along behind him, before Izzy thought of a reply. She ran alongside him. "Who's going to pick up a bunch of kid hitchhikers in the middle of the night? Except maybe some deranged murderer."

"I'm really starting to regret bringing you along, Dizzy."

"You didn't 'bring' me. I just came. What if somebody from Coolidge picks us up, and they know who we are?"

"Calm down. We're not hitching until we get out of Coolidge. Farther up Route 9. Then we wait until we see a truck. Truck drivers will pick up anybody. I'll make sure the driver looks okay before we get in. And we'll have a story ready for him."

"*What* story?"

"Our cover story. I'm thinking we're brothers and sister. Our mother lives in Coolidge, and our dad lives in Eastman. Our dad's expecting us, but . . . our mom's car broke down, so she couldn't drive us there."

Izzy didn't think that made sense. "Why didn't she just call our dad to come get us?"

"She tried to, but his cell phone wasn't on. Or maybe it wasn't charged. He forgets to charge it sometimes."

Izzy shook her head. "What kind of mother

lets her kids hitchhike all over the place at eleven o'clock at night?"

Ben thought that over. "Okay, maybe she's sick. Really sick. And we don't know anybody else in town because we're new here. So we're going to our dad's to get him to come down and take her to the hospital—"

"Because we're too dumb to call 911?" Izzy asked. "That's ridiculous."

Oliver looked back and forth between them as they trudged down the street, waiting to hear the final word on what lie he was supposed to learn.

"Okay," Izzy said. "How about this? Our mother's sick, but not *that* sick. She's coming down with the flu. Our father doesn't charge his phone. We don't want to hang around Flu-ville, so we decided to hitch up to our dad's house. We do it all the time. No big deal."

Ben tilted his head. "It's not that different from *my* story."

"Yours was too complicated. I think it's better if it's simple. We don't need to make it a whole long story."

Ben nodded slowly. "Yeah, okay. You're not a bad liar, Dizzy. Who knew?"

They tried to stay off streets that had lots of streetlights, so nobody would see and recognize them. Ben seemed to know every dark road and alleyway that zigzagged through Coolidge. They were approaching the city limits by the time something Ben said earlier floated back to the top of Izzy's consciousness. She gave him a suspicious look.

"Wait. How come you said our father lives in Eastman?"

Ben shrugged. "I don't know. Just the first place that came to mind."

"And if we're headed west, why are we walking north? Where are we really going?"

"Lake Chautauqua. You know that."

"I mean *first*. Where are we hitchhiking to *now*? Eastman, aren't we? To your uncle Steve's."

Ben looked down at Oliver, and Oliver gave him a guilty smile.

"Sorry," Oliver said. "I told her not to tell anybody, and she didn't."

"She might have, though," Ben said.

Oliver shook his head. "No. I trust Izzy."

Izzy was happy to hear it, but she still wanted an answer. "Tell me the truth, Ben."

He sighed. "Yes, okay, we're going to my uncle Steve's."

Izzy stopped walking. "I don't want to go there! Oliver said he drinks beer and smokes pot."

"Once in a while—not every minute." Ben sounded exasperated. "He's a good guy. The pot is only to help him sleep."

"Your dad doesn't like him," Izzy reminded Ben.

"My dad liked him fine before my mom left. Now he acts like everything that has any connection to her is poisonous."

"What about the tattoos?" Izzy asked. "He's the one who let you get them, isn't he?"

"So what? Everybody has tattoos," Ben said.

"I don't have a tattoo," Oliver said.

Ben smiled at him. "Well, no, you don't. You're only ten."

"And you're only sixteen," Izzy reminded Ben.

"Sixteen in human years," he said. "But a lot older in divorced-parent years."

A grin popped onto Izzy's face, surprising her. She knew exactly what he meant. It was the first thing Ben had ever said that she agreed with completely.

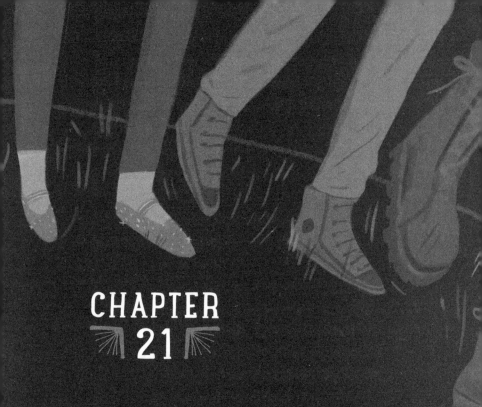

CHAPTER 21

With all the walking, the bandages on Izzy's heels had slipped down into her shoes and were no longer protecting the right places. She didn't want Ben to notice that she was limping, but it was hard to pretend it didn't hurt. Finally she gave in to the pain and began to hobble.

"Why are you walking funny?" Ben asked.

"My shoes are too tight," she admitted.

He'd already gotten the flashlight out, and now he shone it on her silver slippers. "Well, why did you wear *those*? You should have worn sneakers."

"I couldn't. My sneakers are falling apart."

"She was *supposed* to buy sneakers, but she bought those shoes instead," Oliver said. "Aunt Maggie was really mad."

"Oliver, don't be a snitch," Izzy said.

"Well, we're pretty far out of town now," Ben said. "Let's stop for a few minutes and see if any trucks come along. If one does, you two stand closest to the highway, and I'll stand back in the shadows a little bit."

"Why?" Izzy wanted to know. "So if the truck swerves, we get hit first?"

Ben's mouth fell open. "God, why are you so suspicious of me? Have I ever tried to hurt you? We need to get a ride. People are more likely to stop for a girl and a little kid than a teenage boy. That's just the way it is."

Izzy felt bad for saying that about the truck hitting them first, but it was hard for her to apologize to people. Especially to Ben. "I just . . . I don't know. I never hitchhiked before. I don't know how to do it."

"I know you haven't. That's why I'm telling you how to do it," Ben said. "Okay, here comes a car. Get out there."

"But you said it should be a truck—"

"The first one never stops anyway. This is practice."

Stomach churning, Izzy stepped nearer to the

highway and put her arm out straight, her thumb pointed into the air, the way she'd seen people do it in movies. What if the car *did* stop? What if it was somebody she knew? What if they called her mother? What if—?

The car whizzed past without even slowing down.

She was outraged. "They didn't stop!"

Ben shrugged. "Most of them don't. It's not the fastest way to travel."

Three more cars and a big truck passed them by without stopping. Izzy was starting to feel desperate. "Maybe they can't see us," she said.

Ben snorted. "Are you kidding? Your hair's like a lighthouse."

When was he going to stop making fun of her hair? Izzy folded her arms across her chest. "This isn't going to work. Nobody ever stops. We're going to have to walk all the way back home."

"Somebody will stop," Ben said evenly. And then, as if the whole thing had been prearranged, a pickup truck slowed down and pulled onto the gravel shoulder twenty yards up the road.

"Told you," Ben said. "Trucks always stop. Come on!" He ran to the truck, yanked open the door, and peered in. Apparently he liked the looks of the driver well enough. He held the door open so Izzy and then Oliver could climb in. The cab was wide, but it was still a little tight with four of them across, so the driver, a middle-aged man with thick red hair and a two-day beard, suggested that Oliver sit on Izzy's lap. Izzy figured Oliver had probably never ridden in a car without being buckled into a seat belt before. He gripped her arms with his sharp, untrimmed fingernails, looking both thrilled and terrified to find himself in such dangerous circumstances.

"Whatchu kids doing out here so late at night? Kinda dangerous, isn't it?" the driver asked.

Izzy looked at Ben, wondering which of them would recite the lie.

Oliver beat them to it. "Our dad lives in Eastman, and our mom has the flu," he said.

"Is that so?" The driver didn't ask for any more explanation, and none of them offered any. "I can take you to Eastman," he said. "It's right on my way."

"That would be great," Ben said. "Do you know where Steve's Automotive is? We're going to the house right in back of that."

"Sure I do! Steve's a friend of mine. But if he's your dad, he's been keeping secrets from me all these years!" The guy laughed.

Ben gave a nervous laugh. "Well, actually, he's more like my uncle."

The driver put up his hand like a stop sign. "Hey, kid. I ask you no questions—you tell me no lies."

They rode the rest of the way in a friendly silence. The truck driver pulled over in front of Steve's Automotive, and they all got out.

"Thanks," Ben said.

"No problem. Tell Steve that Ronnie says hi. And I'll be waitin' to hear his story about how he all of a sudden got hisself a buncha kids." The driver laughed again and pulled away.

"Well, that lie stunk," Izzy said. "We'll have to come up with something better for next time."

"I already have," Ben said. "So when we get in there, follow my lead, okay?"

Oliver nodded.

"You're going to lie to your uncle?" Izzy asked.

"I have to. It's the only way we'll get a car."

"A *car*! You can't drive!"

Ben put his finger to his lips and whispered, "Yes, I can. Uncle Steve's been teaching me."

"Do you have a license?" Izzy whispered back.

"Not yet, but—"

The door flew open. An enormous man with a thick black beard and tattoos up and down both arms stood in the doorway, resting his massive fists on his hips. "I thought I heard something out here," he said. "Didn't I just see you this afternoon, kiddo? What the hell are you doing here this time of night? I was just about to go to bed."

Izzy wondered if that meant he'd already smoked his bedtime marijuana.

"Hey, Uncle Steve," Ben said. "Can we come in?"

The big man backed up and made a sweeping motion with his hands. "'Course you can. Who've you got with you? Hey, I know. This must be that Oliver you were telling me about."

Oliver stared up at the towering mass of Uncle Steve and nodded.

Ben's uncle stuck out a big paw. "Pleased to meet you, Oliver." Then he extended the same hand to Izzy, while his eyes took in her bright shock of hair. "And who's this colorful little lady?"

"Oh, that's Dizzy," Ben said, as if he'd almost forgotten she was there. "She's Oliver's cousin."

"*Izzy!*" she said as the man's hand enveloped hers.

"Have a seat. Have a seat," Uncle Steve said, motioning them toward a sagging gray couch that had been scratched to pieces, probably by the black cat whose lanky body was stretched across it.

"You hungry?" Uncle Steve asked. "I got some peanuts."

"Sure," Ben said. He shooed the cat off the sofa, and the three of them fell onto it. Oliver slumped against the arm of the couch, barely able to keep his eyes open. Izzy immediately kicked off her shoes, while Ben launched into the story he'd cooked up on the way.

"So, the thing is, Ms. Shepherd, Dizzy's mom, is a nurse at the college and there was some kind of big emergency there tonight, and she got called in to help. So we were alone at the house, and the kids couldn't sleep. They got kind of scared."

"*Kids?*" Izzy piped up. But Ben's cold stare stopped her from saying more.

"So," he continued, "one of my friends gave us a lift up here. I thought we could bunk on your floor tonight, and maybe in the morning you could drive us to school. Is that okay?"

Uncle Steve looked skeptical. "Does Ms. Shepherd know about this plan, Bennie?" He put a big bowl of peanuts in their shells on the coffee table, and Ben grabbed a handful.

Bennie! Izzy let out a half laugh and reached for a peanut. Oh, man, was she glad to know Ben's uncle called him a dumb nickname. She'd put that in her back pocket for later.

"Yeah, yeah," Ben lied. "We called her."

Uncle Steve looked each of them in the face and then said, "The little guy's practically asleep already."

"No, I'm not!" Oliver forced himself to sit up straight.

"I guess it's okay as long as you told the lady

you're staying with. I'm in enough trouble with your dad as it is."

"Yeah, sorry about that," Ben said.

"I got some old sleeping bags in the back. You can stretch out here on the floor."

They took turns in Uncle Steve's grimy bathroom while he found the bags and three flat pillows. Then he brought in three glasses of water and put them on the coffee table. "In case you get thirsty in the middle of the night."

"Thanks," Ben said, downing half his glass immediately.

"Russ sure did a good job on your ink," Uncle Steve said, gesturing to his nephew's arm. "Lemme see the other one."

Ben glanced a little nervously at Izzy, then peeled off his T-shirt so a third tattoo, hidden under his sleeve, was visible. The wolf and the scorpion were both black, but the large bird with enormous wings and tail feathers blazed across Ben's shoulder in bright reds and golds. It looked almost three-dimensional, as though it might fly away at any moment.

"You keep the nicest one hidden," Izzy said. Ben didn't say anything back, but his uncle gave a sharp laugh. Izzy wished she could stare at the bird for a few minutes, but she couldn't do it now, when Ben was standing right next to her, half naked. She didn't want him to think she was interested in his bare chest or his muscly arms. It was this creature drawn so skillfully on his skin that fascinated her.

Izzy didn't believe for one minute that the tattoos held no meaning for Ben, that they were just random signs of rebelliousness. You didn't cover one whole side of your body with any old design. Ben had picked these particular beasts for a reason. One that bites, one that howls, and one that flies.

The new tattoo had caught Oliver's attention too. "Wow! That's even cooler than the scorpion or the wolf! What kind of a bird is it?"

"It's a phoenix," Uncle Steve explained. "From Greek mythology. When the phoenix dies, a new bird rises up out of the ashes of the old one. So in a way, it never dies."

"It's reborn," Ben said.

"It's a reminder that people can start over too, and have a new life," Uncle Steve said.

Oliver leaned forward and gently touched a golden wing. "Are they real?" he asked.

"No," Ben said. "They're kind of a symbol."

"A symbol of hope," Uncle Steve explained. "They remind us not to give up."

"Oh." As he often did these days, Oliver looked wounded. "I wish they were real. I'd like to see one come back to life."

CHAPTER 22

The sleeping bags looked dirty and smelled moldy, but Izzy and Oliver were so tired from their long walk, they fell asleep almost immediately. Whether Ben slept, Izzy didn't know. When he shook her awake before the sun was even up, she groaned. She was still sleepy, and her hip was sore from lying on the hard floor. What the heck was she doing in Eastman, anyway, sleeping in Ben's uncle's stinky sleeping bag? What had seemed like an adventure late last night seemed like an idiotic idea this morning. She wished she were back at home in her own bed.

Oliver was already up, quietly folding his sleeping bag.

Ben put a finger to his lips and whispered to Izzy, "Get your stuff together and grab the sleeping bag, just in case we need it."

"I have to use the bathroom first," Izzy whispered back.

Ben shook his head. "No time. Too noisy. We'll stop somewhere."

"But I *need* to," Izzy said again.

Oliver put his hand on her arm, his face pinched with worry. "Please, Izzy. Let's go while we can. Dad has been gone a whole day already."

Izzy sighed and nodded. She'd come this far—she wouldn't let Oliver down now. She picked up her gear and tiptoed out the back door with the boys. Ben pulled it closed in quiet, incremental clicks.

The leaves that had already fallen made a soft crunchy noise as they walked past a line of dark garages.

"I hope your uncle doesn't wake up," Oliver whispered.

"Don't worry," Ben said. "He usually sleeps late. I told him I'd wake him when we were ready to go to school."

"He was nice to us," Oliver said. "I feel kind of bad about lying to him."

"So do I," Ben admitted. "But I'll explain the whole thing to him later."

"You're going to be in so much trouble," Izzy said.

"Hey, you're in this up to your neck too, Diz," Ben said.

Izzy knew he was right.

Ben went into the last of four garages and opened the trunk of the car parked inside. "Put your stuff back here."

"We're taking a Malibu?" Oliver was impressed.

"This is the car Uncle Steve's been teaching me to drive. It's in good shape. Plus"—Ben reached down and scooped something off the floor in front of the driver's seat—"he always leaves the keys in it."

Izzy sighed. "Now we're stealing a car. I hope I look good in an orange jumpsuit."

"Not stealing," Ben corrected her. "*Borrowing*. I left Uncle Steve a note explaining everything— except where we were going."

"I left a note for Mom too," Izzy said.

"You did? You didn't tell me that." Ben's forehead wrinkled.

"I didn't tell her where we were going—only that we were looking for Uncle Hen. I didn't want her to think we just disappeared overnight."

Ben nodded. "Maybe that's good. They'll be less likely to call the police right away if they aren't so worried."

Izzy figured the grown-ups would still be plenty worried, but she didn't say it out loud. They climbed in, Izzy up front with Ben. He turned the key, and the engine rumbled like thunder in the predawn silence. They all looked toward the house as the car inched out of the garage, but no one came running out.

Izzy grunted as she slipped her shoes off. The blisters on her heels were raw, and they burned even more than they had yesterday.

"I can't believe you wore shoes you can't even walk in," Ben said.

"I can walk," Izzy said. "Just worry about your driving, *Bennie*, so I don't have to walk."

"Let's just go!" Oliver demanded from the back seat.

As Ben made the turn, slowly and carefully, onto Route 9, Izzy glanced at him and saw he was hunched over the steering wheel, his hands holding on to the thing with a death grip. Her stomach did a cartwheel. What in the world were they doing? Was there any chance Ben was really going to be able to drive this car all the way across the state of New York?

She turned around to look at Oliver and was dismayed to see that he seemed to have turned to stone. "Are you buckled in?"

He nodded but continued to stare out the side window, his jaw locked in place.

"Good," Izzy said. "At twenty miles an hour, we ought to be there by the middle of next week."

Ben didn't say anything for a minute, but she saw his chin quiver as he tried not to laugh. After a minute or two she thought she felt him relax a little bit. Finally he leaned back in his seat and said, "I'm getting used to it. It'll be okay. I can do this."

And it turned out, he could. After half an hour, with the sun rising, he'd settled into the job, and they were driving at a more or less normal speed. It helped that there weren't many other cars on the road. In the small towns they passed through, rush hour only meant a few more people going to the post office or dropping their kids off at the regional school.

"Do you know where you're going?" Oliver asked Ben.

"I printed out maps before we left Coolidge so I wouldn't have to have my phone on," Ben said. "I want to stay off the main highways, since I've never actually driven on one before."

"How much driving experience do you really have?" Izzy wanted to know.

"More than you."

"That's not comforting," she said.

"I'll be fine. We can't drive as fast on the smaller roads—that's all." Ben turned partway around to look at Oliver. "But we'll get there, Captain—don't you worry."

Oliver nodded stiffly, but Izzy was pretty sure he wasn't going to stop worrying anytime soon.

As they drove past farms and fields, Izzy fidgeted in her seat. "I really need to use the bathroom," she said.

"I'm looking for a place," Ben said.

The excitement of sneaking off distracted her a little bit. *We're pretty brave,* she thought proudly. Even if Uncle Henderson was perfectly fine out there in his trailer in the woods, Oliver wasn't fine without him, and that wasn't fair. The kid already had too many hard things to deal with for a ten-year-old. Izzy was going to make sure there wasn't one more.

"Look," Ben said, pointing. "There's a diner coming up. We can get gas and breakfast and use the bathroom."

"*Finally,*" Izzy said. Then something occurred to her. "Do you have any money? Because I have four dollars and Oliver has two."

"Yeah, I've got some," Ben said. "I . . . I took money from Uncle Steve's emergency stash."

Izzy's hand flew to her face. "You mean we stole his car *and* his money?"

"He won't be mad. It'll be okay."

"How much did you take?"

"About seventy-five dollars." He turned into the diner parking lot.

"Oh my God!"

"Gas costs money, Dizzy. Did you think cars ran on hopes and dreams? Did you want to have a meal now and then?"

Izzy didn't have an answer for that. Her stomach had been growling since they'd gotten on the road.

Inside the diner, Ben and Oliver got a booth while Izzy hobbled into the bathroom. A teenage girl looked up from washing her hands at a sink, and an explosion of laughter burst out of her. Izzy had to pee so badly that she paid no attention, but afterward, washing her own hands, she looked in the mirror and saw what must have caused the girl's reaction.

Izzy's bright yellow hair, which she'd completely forgotten about, was all smashed down on top, and the chopped-off ends stood out at right angles to her face. She looked like Big Bird after he'd stuck his head in a blender. Plus her clothes looked like they'd been slept in, which of course they had. She was a mess.

She splashed water on her hair and tried to make the spikes stand up again, but she hadn't brought her gel along, and the wet locks fell onto her forehead like pointy yellow teeth. Water dripped down her face and onto her wrinkled

T-shirt. Ben would be sure to make fun of her. But there was nothing to do about it, so she readied herself to face him and walked out.

What she hadn't expected was that the girl she'd seen in the bathroom would have gathered several friends to wait for her exit. The four of them bent over, dissolving in giggles, when they saw Izzy's wet hair.

"Oh my God, you made it *worse!*" the original girl said. "I didn't think that was possible!"

The girls laughed so hard, they held on to each other as they stumbled out the diner door. All the other customers, including Ben and Oliver, turned to see what was so funny. *Izzy* was so funny.

She felt like running out of the diner and getting back in the car, but she wasn't about to let Ben see how humiliated she was. As she walked to the table, people whispered and chuckled, though not quite as rudely as the four girls. She slid into the booth, willing her chin to stop quivering, and looked down at the gigantic plastic menu so she wouldn't have to see the smirk she knew would be on Ben's face.

For a long moment they sat in silence, until Ben said, "Oliver wants pancakes. How about you?"

Had he not seen what happened? That would be a miracle. Izzy cleared her throat, hoping her voice wouldn't come out sounding choked. "Can we afford pancakes?"

"Sure," Ben said. "We'll have a good breakfast, then after this we'll just eat the stuff I brought along."

Izzy was still afraid to look up at Ben, even though he didn't seem to be laughing at her.

"Okay, I'll have pancakes too," she said.

She felt something tap her hand and dared to glance over at Oliver. He looked very serious as he handed her a small black comb. "Here. I had it in my pocket."

That even Oliver felt sorry for her was the last straw. Izzy felt her throat close up, but she gritted her teeth and tightened the muscles around her eyes. The tears were there, but she was *not* going to let them fall. Not in front of Ben.

She blinked to clear her eyes, but that was a mistake. One renegade tear escaped and began a zigzag journey down her cheek. Ben jumped up. "I'll give 'em our order on my way to the bathroom. Pancakes all around."

By the time he returned, Izzy had brushed away the tear and combed her wet hair out of her face. She was amazed that Ben had had no comment on her humiliation, but she was careful not to look him in the face, just in case that inspired one.

They ate their pancakes quickly, filled the gas tank, and got back on the road.

CHAPTER 23

It was a chilly morning, and Izzy was glad she'd brought along her sweatshirt. Although she hadn't particularly noticed the leaves changing in Coolidge, out here in the country, driving past enormous sugar maples and roadside stands of oak and locust, she couldn't pretend that summer wasn't over. The trees hadn't fully turned, of course—it was still early—but whole branches were already red or gold, and some leaves had floated to the ground. The poison ivy that snaked down the gullies toward the creek might fool a city person into taking its pretty scarlet leaves home to press between the pages of a book, but Izzy knew better. Her dad had taught her to recognize the toxic plant from a safe distance.

Autumn, like memories of her father, made Izzy feel sad. Autumn was change you could actually *see*, which was preferable to the kind that blindsided you, but still. It meant something was over and done with, whether you were ready for it or not.

Ben had handed Izzy the maps he'd printed out from the computer, but he'd pretty much memorized their route already, so there wasn't much for her to do. Uncle Steve had left some old CDs in the car, and Izzy played a few of them to fill up the silence, even though she'd never heard of the bands before. Most of them were country and had silly names like Nitty Gritty Dirt Band and the Flying Burrito Brothers.

Around nine o'clock they passed a sign that read, "Welcome to New York, the Empire State."

"Look, Oliver! We're in New York already!" Izzy said. But when she turned to look at him, he seemed to be in the same frozen position he'd been in before. "Are you okay?"

"Stop asking me dumb questions!" he yelled, suddenly coming alive.

Whoa, the kid was flipping out.

"I need to stop at this gas station," Ben said. "I drank too much coffee at the diner."

"Okay. You should pee too, Oliver," Izzy said.

"Stop telling me what to do, Izzy! You aren't my *mother!*" His eyes bulged out of his head as he glared at her.

She was about to say, "Thank God for that," but then she saw the shock on Oliver's face as he realized what had just come out of his mouth, and she remembered that she couldn't say anything the least bit mean about his mother. Not ever.

Ben pulled the car into the station and turned it off. "Hey, Oliver, man, you don't have to go to the bathroom, but it'll do you good to get out of the car and stretch," he said.

"I don't want to keep stopping all the time," Oliver said, though less angrily than before. "I just want to get there as fast as we can."

Ben got out of the car and opened the back door for Oliver. "We're gonna get there—don't you worry about it. But I have to take a few breaks now and then. Okay? I'm not used to driving this much."

Oliver gave a quick nod, then followed Ben and Izzy as they trooped inside to get the keys to the restrooms. His shoulders drooped, but his face stayed hard. Ben stopped at the soda machine before getting back behind the wheel. By the time Izzy got to the car, Oliver was already buckled in again, motionless, eyes focused on the road ahead.

Around noon, Izzy studied Ben's maps. It seemed as though they were just south of Oneonta, which was well into New York State. The distance from home made Izzy simultaneously uncomfortable and excited. She kept imagining what her mother must have done when she walked into her bedroom and found that note. Probably the first thing she did was call Dr. Gustino so the two of them could blow a few gaskets together. And what were they doing now? Was Izzy's disappearance enough of a worry for her mom to call her dad? Was Dr. Gustino on his way home from St. Louis? Had anybody thought to call Uncle Steve? It made Izzy nervous to imagine what must be going on back in Coolidge, or to think about what *would* happen when the three of them got back.

"What do you think your dad will do?" Izzy asked Ben. "I mean, he gets mad pretty easily, doesn't he?"

"He does now," Ben said. "He didn't used to."

"When your mom was around, you mean?"

Ben nodded.

"I guess when she left, you *both* got mad," Izzy said.

He gave her a quick look with his razor-blade

eyes. "We're not the same. I'm nothing at all like my dad."

Izzy turned away and mumbled under her breath, "I wouldn't say *that*."

Ben's voice was icy. "You don't even know me, so don't go thinking you've got me all figured out."

Izzy rolled her eyes. "Believe me, I wouldn't waste my time trying to figure you out."

To stop herself from thinking about the consequences of their getaway, Izzy tried to concentrate on other things. Maybe she could come up with something funny about driving. What would Jerry say? *What's the deal with teenage drivers? They got the music on their phone, they're texting somebody—there's a movie up on a screen in the ceiling, and they're eating pizza and breaking up with their girlfriend at the same time. Multitasking. They do everything simultaneously so when they get home, they can take a nap. I think you should be about forty-five before you get the keys to a car. And preferably married. With an extremely boring life.*

Was forty-five a funny number? She wasn't sure. She could hear Jerry saying the lines and making it sound funny, but it would probably sound stupid in her voice. That was another hard thing about comedy—you had to figure out what your comic identity was, who you were going to be when you stood up in front of the audience. But what was funny about *her* life, except her hairdo?

Of course, Tina Fey said you should make fun of yourself before somebody else had a chance to, so maybe she should work up some Big Bird jokes. The problem was, that still stung too much to seem funny.

"I'm hungry," she said finally, bouncing in her seat. "Can we get out the peanut butter?"

Ben glanced in the rearview mirror. "Okay with you to stop for a few minutes, Oliver?"

Izzy looked into the back seat. Oliver seemed a little calmer than he had before.

"A few minutes," he agreed.

They were on a country road with wide shoulders, so it was easy for Ben to find a place to pull off and stop. "Let's get out to eat," he said. "I need to stand up and walk around a little."

Oliver handed the bag of food out to Ben and Izzy but stayed in the back seat. "I'm good here," he said.

Leaning against the car, Ben used his pocketknife to spread the peanut butter on three slices of bread. He handed Izzy and Oliver their sandwiches, then licked the knife clean.

"Be careful!" Izzy said. "You'll cut your tongue off! And also, ick, that's the only knife we have, and you just got your germs all over it."

"Sorry, Girl Scout. Did you want to go wash it off in the stream?" Ben asked.

"Okay, I will. Where's there a stream?"

"I think we passed one about half an hour ago. Have a nice hike." He folded his sandwich in half and stuck the entire thing in his mouth.

Izzy made a face. "If you choke on that, I'm not giving you the Heimlich."

It took Ben a minute to swallow the wad of bread in his mouth, but then he said, "If you gave me the Heimlich, Dizzy, it would *make* me choke."

"How come you two argue so much?" Oliver yelled out the window.

"Because we're different," Ben said.

"Because he's annoying," Izzy said.

"I don't think you're that different," Oliver said. "And you're both kind of annoying the way you pick on each other all the time. Couldn't you try to get along better?"

Izzy could feel her ears get hot, and she didn't look at Ben.

But Ben looked in the window at Oliver. "It bothers you, doesn't it?"

Oliver nodded. "All that arguing makes my stomach hurt. It would be easier if we were all . . . friends."

"Okay," Ben said. "For you, Captain Hook, I'll do my best."

"Okay," Oliver said seriously as he peeled a banana.

"Whatever," Izzy said. She finished off the water from her bottle.

"You drank all your water already?" Ben said.

"Well, I didn't have a big Coke back there like you did." Izzy would have said something about how selfish it was to buy a soda for yourself without getting one for anybody else, but she glanced at Oliver and kept her mouth shut.

Ben didn't argue either. "Right," he said. "I forgot that."

They stood at the side of the road for another ten minutes, the crunch of potato chips the only sound. It was going to be a long, silent car ride, Izzy thought, if she had to be nice to Ben the whole way.

"So, Oliver," Ben said, once they were back on the road, "has Liam been okay lately? He hasn't been calling you dumb names or anything, has he?"

"Not as much," Oliver said. "He mostly just ignores me, which I don't mind. I mean, *most* of the kids in my class ignore me."

"Not Suzanne, though," Izzy said. "She likes you."

"Who's Suzanne?" Ben asked, glancing at Oliver in the mirror. "You didn't tell me about her."

Izzy was glad she knew at least one thing Ben didn't.

"She's just this girl in my class," Oliver said. "She's okay."

"She was sitting and waiting with Oliver when I picked him up after school yesterday," Izzy explained. "I thought she might have a little crush on him."

Oliver groaned. "*No*. You want to know why Suzanne hangs out with me? Because her older sister died last year, and nobody wants to be friends with her now either."

"What?" Izzy turned sideways in her seat. "Her sister died? How?"

Oliver shrugged. "I don't know. Some kind of cancer. She doesn't like to talk about it."

"That's awful," Izzy said.

"Yeah, and now her parents argue all the time and might even get a divorce. So her life sucks almost as bad as mine."

"But that's no reason for the other kids not to be friends with you guys," Ben said.

"They think it is. They think death is like the flu, and they don't want to catch it."

Ben nodded. "Kids can be really mean to each other."

"Were your friends mean to you when your mom left?" Oliver asked him.

Izzy looked over at Ben and instantly wished she hadn't. The color drained out of his face, and his Adam's apple bobbed in his throat. His spark had disappeared. The brat had left the building.

The answer to Oliver's question was obviously a painful one, and Izzy tried desperately to think of something funny to say to save them all from whatever memories were attacking Ben.

But suddenly there was something more important to worry about. "What the hell is *that*?" Ben said, staring out the windshield.

"We're on fire!" Oliver yelled.

Smoke seemed to be belching out from under the hood of the Chevy. "Pull over! Pull over!" Izzy screamed.

Ben steered the car off the road as soon as he could find a spot to do it. "Get out, both of you!" he said. "In case it blows up!"

They jumped out of the car and ran down into a gully. Standing beneath some pine trees, they watched the smoke drift out from under the hood. It didn't seem to be getting any worse, but it wasn't stopping either. After a few minutes, Ben walked back and slowly lifted the hood.

"Be careful!" Izzy shouted.

"I don't think this is smoke," Ben said. "It doesn't smell like smoke."

Izzy and Oliver came a little closer. "Well, whatever it is, we can't drive it that way," Izzy said.

Ben kicked the bumper. "Crap."

Oliver's face melted. "We have to fix it," he said. "We have to find my dad."

"I know," Ben said, putting a hand on the boy's shoulder. "It's okay. I've got my phone. I'll find a place to get it fixed." He fished the phone out of his back pocket and turned it on.

"God, there are about a hundred missed calls and voice mails from my dad on here. And a few from Dizzy's mom too."

"Don't listen to them now," Izzy said.

"Don't intend to," Ben said. In a minute or two, he had located the nearest auto repair shop and called.

Izzy couldn't understand much from only listening to Ben's side of the conversation. He described what the smoke looked like and where he thought it might be coming from, and then he just listened for a long time. Izzy paced back and forth, careful not to look at Oliver.

"Okay. Thanks a lot," Ben said finally. He hung up and turned the phone off again.

"Well?" Izzy asked. "What's happening?"

"He says it's probably the antifreeze leaking out—this is vapor, not smoke. I guess it happens with these old Malibus because of the way they're designed." He pointed to something under the hood. "See, the intake manifold—"

"Just tell me what we're supposed to do now," Izzy said. "Can we fix it?"

"Well, *we* can't, but the guy's coming to tow us in."

"*Tow* us?"

"Well, what did you think, Dizzy? That we could push the car to the next town?"

Ben and Izzy realized at the same time that they were raising their voices with each other again. They both turned guiltily to look at Oliver. The boy stared silently at Ben's face, probably looking for some scrap of hope or good news.

"I'm sorry, Oliver," Ben said, "but this shouldn't take too long. A couple of hours probably."

"Do we have enough money to pay for it?" Izzy was almost afraid to ask.

"I don't know," Ben said.

"We shouldn't have had the pancakes," Izzy said.

Ben looked at Oliver. "Don't worry, Captain Hook. We'll figure it out."

"Are you okay, Oliver?" Izzy asked.

"Stop asking me that!" He backed away from them until he was under the trees again, then he sat down, pulled up his legs, and let his head fall heavily onto his bony knees.

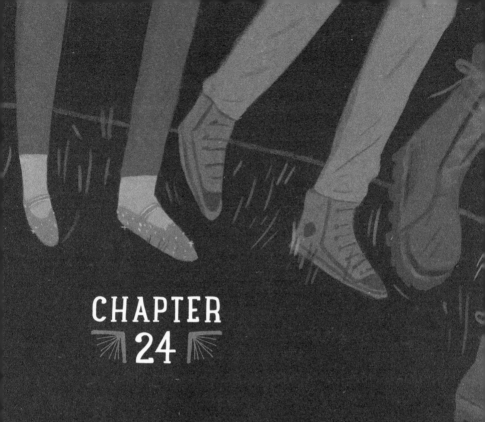

CHAPTER 24

Twenty-five minutes later they were sitting in the cab of Ellis Canty's tow truck, dragging the Malibu behind them. Izzy had called him Mr. Canty, and he'd corrected her.

"Nobody calls me Mister," he said. "Call me Ellis, unless you're gonna call me somethin' worse!" He had a laugh like a kindly donkey's.

Izzy couldn't stop staring at the man's greasy hands on the steering wheel. She'd never seen such dirty fingernails in her life. Still, she thought Ellis was okay. She'd noticed the way he had blinked twice as he took in her colorful hairdo, but then he'd smiled without commenting on it one way or the other.

"Aren't you guys a little young to be taking a road trip all by yourselves?" Ellis asked.

"I'm eighteen," Ben said before either of the others could speak.

Ellis looked over at him. "Huh. I would have said a little younger, but I can see it now. This your brother and sister?"

"Yeah," Ben said, and no one contradicted him.

Oliver was stuffed between Izzy and Ben on the seat, and she could feel how tense he was. He sat there like a little robot, stiff as steel, staring out the front window. She tried to find his hand with hers, but when she touched him, his fingers were ice cold, and he pulled away from her. Obviously he intended to remain frozen.

"I'm a fan of these old Malibus myself. I don't usually see kids driving them, though," Ellis said once they were back at the shop and his head was under the hood of the car.

"It's my uncle's car," Ben said. "How long will it take to fix it?"

"Well, it's a coolant leak, like I figured," Ellis said.

"Is that expensive?" Izzy asked.

"Don't worry," Ellis said. "I won't overcharge you."

Ben took his wallet out. "The thing is, we've only got fifty-three bucks on us."

"Plus my four dollars," Izzy reminded him.

"And my two," Oliver said.

"So, fifty-nine, I guess," Ben said.

"No credit cards?" Ellis asked.

Ben shook his head.

Ellis seemed to consider this. "Huh. Well, the job would come in at a little more than that, but I'll make you a deal. My wife says if I don't finish mowing that field today, she's gonna make me go to my niece's piano recital with her on my one day off." He pointed out the window to the acreage behind the shop, where a lawnmower stood stalled between foot-high weeds and the smooth green carpet he'd already cut.

"See, we live right over there," he said, pointing to a small house at the edge of the field. "So my wife looks out the window, and it bugs her. She's the kind of person likes everything real neat and clean."

Izzy wondered how anybody who liked things clean could possibly be married to Ellis Canty, who was wiping his filthy fingers on the T-shirt that stretched tightly over his belly.

"I woulda finished the job today if you hadn't called—"

Ben interrupted him. "I'll cut the grass. It won't even take me that long."

Ellis nodded. "Fifty dollars, you cut the grass, and we're even. That'll leave you a few bucks to get where you're going. Which is where, by the way?"

"We're finding my dad," Oliver said. "Way on the other side of New York."

"Our dad . . . he's, umm . . . having car trouble too," Ben said, handing Ellis the fifty dollars.

"Huh. I guess your family's having a rough day," Ellis said. "The mower's got plenty of gas in it. You gotta pull hard to get it started."

"Okay. They can hang around in here, can't they?" Ben asked.

"Sure. Sure. There's a soda machine in the office if you're thirsty," Ellis said.

Ben reached into his pocket and pulled out some change, which he handed to Izzy. "Here. Do you guys mind sharing a drink?"

Izzy shook her head.

"Thanks, Ben," Oliver said quietly. Izzy thought she ought to thank him too, but she couldn't quite bring herself to do it. Some stubbornness wouldn't let the words come out.

Ellis got right to work on the car. Izzy and Oliver sat in the office, drinking their soda and staring out the window as Ben pushed the mower back and forth through the field. Before long he took off his hoodie and left it behind on the mowed grass.

"I like Ben," Oliver said.

"I know you do."

"He's not really a scorpion. He just pretends to be."

Izzy had to admit Ben was not the terrible person her friends thought he was. He wasn't as bad as she'd thought at first either. She didn't know why he was willing to do so much to help Oliver, but day after day he kept doing it, and even though Izzy felt a little jealous of how much her cousin liked him, she was starting to understand it too.

She wondered if it was the same with Dr. Gustino. He seemed kind of crabby and unhappy to Izzy, but maybe that was just what you saw first. Maybe her mom had spent enough time with him to see the good parts too.

They watched Ben work, as if by watching they could add their energy to his, help push the mower a little bit faster. But as their eyes followed the mower, it suddenly stopped moving, and Ben leaped away from it, his arms thrown wide. For a minute Izzy was reminded of the mime who'd followed them on the street in Coolidge, the way he exaggerated his movements, trying to be funny. But she knew immediately this was no joke. Even from this distance she could see the look of shock on Ben's face. He slapped at his neck and his arms, and then he started to run, tearing off his T-shirt and throwing it aside as if it were on fire.

"Ellis! Come here! There's something wrong!" Izzy yelled.

The man stuck his head into the office and saw immediately what was going on outside the window.

"Dammit! Ground hornets!" Ellis banged out the back door and ran toward Ben, who was headed right for him. "Drop trou! Get your clothes off!" Ellis yelled.

Izzy and Oliver stood at the window, transfixed by the picture of Ellis swatting at bees and helping Ben rip off his shoes and jeans. Once Ben was down to boxer shorts, Ellis pulled him inside, a few hornets coming through the door with them. Ellis clapped his big hands around the last few invaders, and they dropped to the floor of the shop.

"I'm so sorry, son," Ellis said as he looked Ben over. "You're not allergic, are you?"

Ben held his arms away from his body and stood motionless, stunned. "What? No, I don't think so. What *were* those things?"

"Ground hornets. Some people call 'em yellow jackets. You musta run over a nest with the mower. I thought I got rid of 'em last year, but I guess they came back. Hurts, don't it?"

Ben grimaced. "Yeah. I got stung about a million times."

"Well, twenty, anyway," Ellis said, taking Ben gently by the arm. "I got a shower back in here. You need to wash the stings real good with soap to get out as much of the venom as you can. Then we'll ice 'em down."

Venom? Izzy thought only snakes had venom. Neither she nor Oliver could stop staring at Ben, who stumbled a little as Ellis led him away. Already there were red welts rising on his arms and back. For a minute Izzy thought she might cry, but when she looked at Oliver and saw that he already *was* crying, she swallowed back her own tears.

"He'll be okay," she said, hoping it was true. "It's just bee stings. He's not allergic." Did they know that for sure?

Oliver's swollen eyes looked into hers. "But he's hurt. How's he going to drive? And the car's not even fixed. And—"

"I'm just gonna stand here in the doorway, kid," Ellis yelled into the shower room, "in case you have trouble breathing or anything. If you feel weird, call out, hear me?"

Oliver's dam burst, and he collapsed onto the oily concrete floor, sobbing.

"I'm fine!" Ben called from the shower. "Tell Oliver I'm fine."

Izzy didn't bother to repeat the message. Just saying it wouldn't make it true anyway. She got Ben's duffel bag out of the trunk of the car and found a T-shirt for him, but he hadn't brought another pair of jeans.

While Ben dried off, Ellis ran up to his house and got a bag of frozen vegetables and a pair of his jeans for Ben to wear. The pants were miles too big for him, so Ellis ran a piece of rope through the belt loops to hold them up. Then he darted out the door and scooped up Ben's sneakers, checking first to make sure there were no hornets hiding inside, and the cell phone that had gone flying out of Ben's pocket. "I'll get the rest of your clothes later, after the hive settles down," he said.

Oliver stood looking out the window, tear trails on his face. "The sun's going down," he said mournfully.

Ben sat on a folding chair, holding the bag of peas on his neck, where several of the worst bites were, right in the middle of his howling-wolf tattoo. "Is the car done?" he asked Ellis.

Ellis sighed. "Okay, here's what we're gonna do. I was thinking about it while you were in the shower. The car isn't fixed yet. I got another hour or so to go on it, and it's getting dark already. Besides which, you shouldn't be driving anywhere tonight. Sometimes you get a reaction even a few hours later from that many bites. You need to stay quiet and see how you feel tomorrow."

Ben jumped up. "Tomorrow? We can't stay here all night!"

"Well, you don't really have a choice, do ya?" Ellis said kindly. "Here's what I'm thinking. My brother Andy's got a motel about five miles from here. He'll let you stay there, no charge, when I tell him what happened. He's never full-up anyway. And if there's a problem later on tonight, he'll know who to call. I feel kinda responsible, kid, and I'd be a lot happier knowing you were staying the night there. You can call your parents and tell 'em Ellis is taking good care of ya. Or, if you want, I'll call 'em."

"That's okay, Ellis," Izzy said. "We'll call."

Ben seemed to have shrunk inside the enormous pants. He looked at Oliver. "I'm sorry, Oliver. I know I promised you we'd get there today."

Oliver wouldn't look at him, which Izzy thought wasn't fair. After all, Ben had only been trying to help. It wasn't his fault there were hornets in the ground. And now he was stung all to pieces, which must hurt like the dickens. Just imagining it made Izzy squirm.

"Come on, Oliver, it's not that big of a deal," she said. "If it's today or tomorrow, we'll get there and we'll find him and he'll just be sitting around writing songs. You know how he gets when he's writing. He won't even know what day it is!"

Oliver wouldn't look at either of them.

They all got back into Ellis's truck, Oliver on Izzy's lap so he wouldn't bump into Ben's stung shoulder. The sun was barely visible above the line of trees along the highway.

"Tell you what," Ellis said. "Let's stop on the way, and I'll get you a pizza to take to the motel. You guys must be starving."

Ben and Oliver were silent as gravestones, so Izzy rose to the occasion. "That would be great, Ellis. Thanks a lot."

"Hey," Oliver said, trying to look over his shoulder. "We're going back the way we came!"

"That's where the motel is," Ellis said. "It's not too far."

"But it's backward!" Oliver yelled.

"Oliver!" Izzy shook him, just a little bit, or maybe more than a little bit. "It's okay. We're going to get there. Ben promised you and . . . and I promise you too. We'll find him tomorrow."

"*Tomorrow!*" Oliver wailed. And Izzy knew he was afraid tomorrow would never come.

CHAPTER 25

"Turn it off! It's all stupid!" Oliver said.

He wasn't wrong. All they could find on the motel TV were local news channels and reruns of sitcoms that hadn't been very good the first time around. Izzy hit the power button and the picture disappeared. Lying on one of the two double beds, Oliver turned his back to her.

"I get this bed to myself," he muttered.

"No, you don't," she said. "I'm sleeping there too. Ben needs his own bed."

"You can sleep on the floor, then."

"Oliver, I know you're upset, but stop being so bratty."

"Don't tell me what to do." He pulled the covers up over his head.

Things could be worse, Izzy told herself. At least they had a free place to stay for the night, and Ellis had gotten them an enormous pepperoni pizza for dinner (which Oliver had barely touched). And Ellis had promised to have the car done first thing in the morning and to come back and pick them up. They'd be able to get an early start and finish the drive across New York by mid-afternoon. If Ben was feeling okay. If the car didn't break down again. If their parents hadn't called the police by then. If they could actually find Uncle Henderson at Lake Chautauqua. She didn't want to imagine what Oliver would do if they didn't find him. And, of course, the longer this took, the more worried her mother would be, which meant by the time Izzy finally called her, she'd be just that much more furious.

Ben had gone outside to take a walk, and when he came back into the room he was accompanied by a gust of chilly wind. He'd had a discouraged look on his face ever since the hornets stung him, and Izzy was sorry to see that the walk hadn't erased it.

"Is Oliver asleep?" he asked.

"I don't think so," Izzy said.

Oliver's muffled voice emerged from beneath the blanket. "Yes, I am."

Ben sighed. "I called Uncle Steve."

"You did?" Izzy steeled herself to hear the story.

"I felt bad about tricking him and taking the car and the money."

"What did he say?"

"He was okay about it. He's a good guy. Of course, my dad called him right away this morning and blamed him for everything. I guess my dad and your mom are completely freaking out."

"What did he tell them?"

Ben sat carefully on the other bed. "He admitted we'd come to see him, but he told them he didn't know we planned to take his car. Dad didn't believe him, of course."

"Did your uncle say anything about my mom?"

"Apparently your mom decided we were going to Wilton, which is where she thinks Henderson is—so chances are she's driving there as we speak. Uncle Steve said she wanted to call the police, but my dad talked her out of it—for now, at least."

"Oh my God, I'm so dead." Izzy closed her eyes.

"*You*? I was already on house arrest before this even started. Now my dad is flying back from St. Louis, leaving my sick grandmother behind, and probably trying to come up with a punishment that's bad enough for an underage kidnapper." Ben made slow circles with his stung arm, testing for pain.

"Kidnapper? You're not a kidnapper."

"Apparently your mother has used that word."

Oh my God, her mother must be *furious* if she said something like that about Ben. When Ben was staying with them, she acted like he was some kind of gift from heaven—and now she was calling him a criminal? "You're not that much older than we are, and anyway, we wanted to come," Izzy said. "You didn't make us. It was Oliver's idea to find his father!"

"Oliver is ten. I'm sixteen. I'm supposed to be the smart one." He sighed and pushed up off the bed. "I really thought we could do this. Oliver depended on me, and I'm letting him down."

"No, you aren't. It's not your fault you got stung—"

"That's not how Oliver sees it. I screwed things up, like I always do. And when we get back, my dad's gonna kill me. And if he doesn't, your mom will."

"I'll tell her," Izzy said. "You certainly didn't kidnap *me*. I can make my own decisions!"

Ben glanced at her hair and allowed himself a tiny grin. "I think you proved that." He looked so defeated that Izzy didn't even get mad. In fact, she was glad if her stupid hair made him feel a little better.

When Ellis had gotten the frozen peas from his house, he'd also picked up a box of baking soda. He'd told Ben to mix it with water until it made a paste and then paint it onto his stings to help with the pain and itching. Ben got a glass from the bathroom and watered down the baking soda. He pulled off his T-shirt and stuck his finger in the glass, then dabbed the paste onto the raised lumps that he could reach on his arms and ankles. Izzy saw that both the scorpion and the wolf had been stung, which was pretty weird, but she was glad to see that the phoenix had escaped the attack.

Every time Ben touched one of the stings, he clenched his jaw, and Izzy couldn't stop herself from watching the undisguised pain. The fact that he was enduring all this for Oliver had washed away what was left of her resentment of him.

"Do you want me . . . Should I do the ones on your back?" Izzy asked.

Ben seemed startled by the idea. "Um, you don't have to."

"I know I don't *have* to, but Ellis said the baking soda makes them feel better. You have to sleep tonight so you can drive tomorrow."

He seemed to think it over, then nodded. "Yeah. That's true. Okay." He handed Izzy the glass and sat on the bed with his back to her.

Izzy got a big glob of paste on her finger, then

hesitated. She could see Ben's whole body tense up, waiting for her finger to land on him. He expected her to hurt him, she realized. Not on purpose, not out of meanness, but still, he expected her touch to be painful. It seemed to her that a completely different Ben sat there in front of her, not the tattooed tough guy he wanted everybody to see, but a boy who expected people to hurt him. Izzy was determined her touch would be gentle.

"I'm going to do the one on your neck first," she said, so he'd know what to expect. He nodded. As lightly as she could, she spread the white goo on his swollen red skin. He twitched, but only a little.

"Is that okay? Did it hurt?" she asked.

"No. Not much." His voice was quiet.

"I'm glad you didn't get stung on the phoenix tattoo," Izzy said. "I like that one."

"You do? I thought you hated them all."

"I guess I'm getting used to them," Izzy admitted. "One that bites, and one that howls, and one that . . . one that starts over."

Ben nodded. "Yeah."

"Okay. There are three bites right in the middle of your back," she said before slathering more paste over those. A shiver ran across Ben's shoulders, but this time he didn't twitch. By the time Izzy finished with the nine bites that decorated his back, Ben had relaxed.

"Thanks," he said as he took the glass back from her.

Then, before she thought about it too much, Izzy said, "You *are* the smart one, Ben."

He looked at her, puzzled. "What?"

"You said our parents would be mad at you because you're supposed to be the smart one. You *are* the smart one. I couldn't have figured this all out. I mean, what stuff to bring along, and how to get to this lake we're going to, and what to do when we had car trouble. All of it. You're the smart one."

Ben shook his head and smiled wide. Izzy was pretty sure it was the first time she'd seen him smile a *real* smile and not a mean one or a sarcastic one. At least when he was looking at her.

"Hey, you're not so dumb yourself, Izzy," he said.

She was positive it was the first time he'd called her Izzy.

"You know what? I'm gonna do you a favor too," Ben said. He went to his backpack and searched through one of the side pockets. "I happen to have just what you need."

"I don't need anything."

Ben held up a pair of scissors. "Yes, you do."

"So you're going to stab me with your big scissors?" But she smiled as she said it.

"I'm going to make you look slightly less demented." He pointed to her head.

Izzy's hands flew to her hair. "What? No! You can't!"

"Yeah, actually, I can. It's the one useful thing my mom taught me. I know how to cut hair. She even let me cut hers sometimes."

"But you're a boy!" She knew that was a stupid thing to say, but she was so shocked by Ben's suggestion.

"A lot of men cut hair. A couple of guys worked in the salon with my mom."

Izzy stood up and backed across the room. "I don't need a haircut!"

"You do, Izzy. I'll make it look better—I promise." Quietly he said, "It really couldn't look any worse."

Izzy let her hands drop to her sides. She'd trusted Ben enough to get into a car with him and drive across a whole state. Besides, he was right about her hair—it looked horrible. She flopped into the desk chair and sighed. "Go ahead. Carve Big Bird."

"Hey, I'm gonna give the Bird some style, kid. Just wait." Ben got a towel from the bathroom and draped it around her shoulders. When he made the first cut, Izzy flinched, just as he had when she'd smeared the baking soda on the first of his wounds. Of course, a haircut didn't hurt like hornet stings did, but Izzy was nervous anyway. Still, she willed herself to calm down. She hardly recognized the forlorn, hornet-stung hairdresser who stood behind her. And she didn't want to scare this new Ben away.

Ben didn't talk while he worked. He seemed to be concentrating on the job. At one point he gave a little grunt, and Izzy got worried. "What's wrong? Did you make a mistake?"

"No. You made the mistake when you chopped up your hair like this. I can't fix everything. Why did you do this, anyway?"

"Lots of girls dye their hair!" Which she knew was not really an answer to the question.

"Maybe so, but they don't do it by themselves so the color's all blotchy. And they don't attack themselves with the scissors so it looks like they've been electrocuted."

He was *still* insulting her—she should have known he hadn't really changed. But just as she was about to pull away and tell him to stop, Ben said, "I guess I know why you did it. Same reason I got the tattoos."

Huh. He was right. "So I wouldn't be invisible," she said.

"Yeah. How'd that work out for you?"

"Well, everybody noticed me—"

"I'm sure they did," Ben said with a laugh.

"But not in a good way. In fact, my best friends, Pauline and Cookie, don't even want to hang out with me anymore."

"That's pretty rotten of them."

"Yeah. And they told me some bad stuff about you too."

"Like what?"

"Like, once you hit a guy with a baseball bat and gave him a concussion."

Ben stopped cutting. "What? You didn't believe that, did you?"

Izzy hung her head. "I wasn't sure."

"Izzy, I never did anything like that! People start these dumb rumors—"

"I know. I believe you." She should have said it before, and she had to say it now: "I'm . . . sorry."

He pulled her head back up. "For what?"

"For believing them. And for treating you . . . kind of lousy."

"Yeah, well, I acted kind of lousy," Ben admitted, "so I guess we're even."

"I'm really mad at Cookie and Pauline for saying that stuff. They don't even know you!"

"Sometimes people talk without thinking first," Ben said as he worked to even up the back of her hair. "My old friends were so annoying after my mom left—they said all kinds of dumb stuff, like

"Who needs her?" and "You're better off without her." They acted like it was no big deal to have your mother run away from you. They didn't understand why I was in a bad mood all the time. They thought I should still be the same person I was before, but I wasn't. So I found other people to hang with."

"The ones your dad doesn't like?" She said it quietly, hoping he wouldn't get mad.

For a minute Ben was silent, but then he said, "We took my dad's car one night. Just to ride around for a while."

"Did you drive it?"

He nodded. "Some of the guys were drinking, but I wasn't. Believe me, Uncle Steve has drilled that into me so hard—no drinking and driving. But the cops pulled us over because one of the taillights was out, of all the dumb things. Of course, I didn't have a license . . . and you can imagine the rest."

"That's why you're grounded?"

"Yeah. That's why I figured my dad wouldn't want to get the police involved this time. Twice in a month wouldn't be good. I'll probably never get a real driver's license now."

"Wow." Izzy had a lump in her throat from listening to Ben's story. What was wrong with her lately? Everything made her feel sad.

"Okay. That's the best I can do. What do you think?" Ben whipped the towel off her shoulders, and Izzy turned to look at herself in the mirror.

The chicken feathers were gone. Izzy had layers now and punky little bangs, with a few holes that Ben couldn't quite disguise. Her hair was still bright yellow, of course, but she no longer looked silly. In fact, she looked kind of amazing.

"See, I told you I know what I'm doing. My mom was a good hairdresser. She used to—" He stopped short when he saw the tears running down Izzy's cheeks. "What's wrong?"

"Thank you," Izzy said. Then she ran into the bathroom and slammed the door.

CHAPTER
⊐⊩ 26 ⊪⊏

Izzy tramped through the forest, snow up to her knees. Her job, she knew, was to knock the heavy snow off the branches of the smaller trees before the weight of it could break them. And she did that as quickly as she could, but there were so many trees, and so much snow, and it kept on falling.

It was the bed shaking that woke Izzy up. At first she thought it must be an earthquake, but once her eyes were open and she remembered where she was, she could tell that the only thing moving was Oliver. He was groaning as he thrashed in the bed, throwing himself from side to side, his head crashing around on the pillow.

Izzy put her hands on his shoulders. "Oliver, you're having a nightmare," she whispered, hoping Ben wouldn't wake up too.

Oliver's eyes flew open, but he still didn't seem to be awake. He stared at Izzy as if he'd never seen her before.

"It's okay," she whispered again. "You were dreaming. I was too."

Oliver sat up and looked around the dark room. He made a strangled noise deep in his throat. Izzy watched his face fold in on itself as the sound grew bigger and louder until it became a scream that seemed to have been dragged up from a hole deep inside him. The whole room echoed with the mournful explosion.

The shriek cut right through Izzy and left her breathless. She sat up and scooted across the bed until she was on her knees next to her cousin. She put her arms around his back and tried to pull him toward her, but he resisted. "Oliver, it's okay!" she said again, even though she knew it wasn't and might never be.

And then Ben was beside the bed, though Izzy hadn't heard him get up. He sat on Oliver's other side and took the younger boy's hand in both of his own. "Oliver, don't," he whispered. "Please don't."

When the scream finally ended, a terrifying silence surrounded them, which felt as ominous as the eruption that had come before it. *Where is Uncle Henderson?* Izzy thought angrily. But then she pushed that thought away. She was the one sitting here next to Oliver—she would take care of him. A moment later the quiet was broken by gulping sobs that sounded as much like retching as crying. Oliver threw himself at Izzy like a wild, furious animal, and she tried her best to hold him together.

"I want my *mother!*" he screamed in her face. "I *need* her! Where *is* she? I want my family back!" His crying was half misery and half rage. It cut right into Izzy's heart, and she didn't think she could bear it. Oliver's loss felt like *her* loss, and tears once again streamed down her cheeks. It *wouldn't* be okay for Oliver, or for her either.

But Ben was there too, and his arms gathered them both in. It was too dark to see, of course, but Izzy felt Ben's body shaking next to hers. He was crying too. They sat together like that for a long time. Oliver was the last to stop crying, his sobs gradually turning into a more regular kind of tears and finally becoming deep, heavy, choking breaths. Izzy felt sore all over, as if she'd been ripped apart and put back together incorrectly.

Still, they did not let go of each other. In the

congested, waterlogged silence that followed, Ben whispered, "Oliver, this is your family. *We're* your family." And Izzy nodded because she couldn't speak.

Then the three of them lay back down on the double bed, Oliver in the middle where they could protect him, and slept until morning.

CHAPTER
27

Izzy and Ben woke up to the sound of Oliver blowing his nose. They all padded around the room silently, as if there were someone else still asleep they were afraid to wake up. They took turns in the bathroom without argument. Izzy showered off the stray yellow hairs from the previous night's haircut and stared at her new, almost stylish appearance in the foggy mirror before getting dressed and limping back into the bedroom.

Ben and Oliver sat side by side on the bed, their backpacks ready to go. Ben looked at his phone and said, "Twenty-two text messages from my dad," then turned it off and slipped it back into his pocket without reading them.

Izzy noticed the swelling had gone down on the stings on Ben's arms, at least the ones she could see. While she was looking at his arms, Ben was looking at her feet.

"You're still limping. Take your shoes off, and let me see."

"It's okay. I get used to it as the day goes on," Izzy said.

"Let me see your feet," he repeated.

She flopped onto the bed and kicked off her left shoe. "This is the worst one." There was an oozing blister on her big toe, and the back of her heel looked a little bit like ground beef.

Oliver leaned over to take a look. "Yuck!"

Ben recoiled too. "God, Izzy! You can't wear those shoes!"

"I ran out of Band-Aids. If we can stop somewhere and get a few, I'll be fine."

Their conversation was interrupted by Ellis's knock on the door. He grinned hugely when he saw that Ben was okay.

"We're gonna stop at my favorite diner on the way back to the garage. Breakfast's on me."

"We've got some money left," Ben said. "You don't have to—"

"Oh, yes, I do," Ellis said. "I feel terrible about

you gettin' all stung up yesterday. And anyway, my wife told me I have to, so no arguments."

Izzy and Ben each devoured a plateful of bacon and eggs, and even Oliver ate more than usual. A police cruiser pulled into the parking lot just as they were walking out the diner door. Izzy and Ben shot each other nervous glances over Oliver's head, but the officers just nodded and said hello as they passed by. Their parents had obviously not called the police yet, but Izzy wondered if that would soon change.

When they got back to Ellis's garage, the car was parked outside, ready to go.

"I filled your tank," Ellis said. "And here's twenty bucks back. I'm only charging you for the part, not my labor."

"Really?" Ben asked. "Are you sure?"

Ellis grinned. "After what you went through with those dang hornets? I should be paying you."

"Thanks, Ellis," Ben said. "You've been a big help."

"Don't mention it. Nice meetin' you all," he said. "Not often I see a family where the kids get along as well as you three do." Ellis stuck out his dirt-creased hand and they all shook it.

It was good to be back on the road again. In fact, Izzy thought it was better than good. Something had happened last night. Something awful and then something kind of great. They were a team now, the three of them, and today was the day they were going to find Uncle Henderson and bring him home.

They'd only gone a few miles when Ben turned the car off the highway onto a side street. Oliver noticed immediately.

"How come we turned? Is this the right way?"

"Don't worry. We're making a short detour. It'll only take a few minutes."

"How come? Where are we going?" he asked anxiously.

"Trust me," Ben said, and apparently Oliver did because he sat back in the seat.

A strip mall appeared just ahead of them, and Ben turned into the lot. Okay, Izzy got it now.

"Are we stopping for Band-Aids?" she asked.

"Not exactly, but you're close." Ben's lip turned up at one corner, as if he had a secret. He parked the car and pointed to the store in front of them. "We're going in there."

"A Goodwill store? Why?"

"Shoes."

Ben jumped out of the car, and Izzy and Oliver followed. Izzy had gone with her mother to drop things off at Goodwill, but she'd never shopped there before. She was amazed to see the racks of sneakers, all arranged according to size.

"How did you know this place was here?" Izzy asked.

"I asked Ellis while you were in the bathroom at the diner. He noticed you were wearing stupid shoes too."

While Izzy looked over the possibilities, Ben walked off and came back with a pair of purple socks. "Try them on with these," he said. The second pair Izzy put on, dark gray with pink swirls on the sides, fit perfectly. She jogged up and down the aisle in them.

"They're all broken in already," she said. "And I even like the way they look!"

"Great," Ben said. When she stopped moving, he reached down and pulled off the price tag. "Keep 'em on. You might as well throw those other torture devices in the trash."

"How much are they?" Izzy asked.

"Six bucks. Plus another one for the socks."

"That's all? Seven dollars? I can't believe it!" At which point Izzy realized that even though seven dollars wasn't much money for a pair of socks and shoes, especially shoes that felt good and were kind of cute besides, she didn't *have* seven dollars.

When she told Ben, he said, "I know. We're using Uncle Steve's money. This is an emergency, Izzy. We don't have a choice here. You can't spend another day ruining your feet with shoes that don't fit."

Izzy got quiet. Ben had said "we" didn't have a choice, as if her feet were his business now, as if what hurt her hurt him too. Had anyone besides her mother (and maybe, a few years back, her father) ever felt that way about her?

"See, that didn't take long," Ben said, once they were back in the car. "Ten minutes, maybe."

"Fifteen," Oliver said. "Now no more stops!"

"Aye, aye, Captain Hook," Ben said.

And suddenly the miles seemed to fly by, even though Ben wasn't driving any faster than he had the day before.

"Do you ever listen to stand-up comedy?" Izzy was surprised she'd asked out loud the question that had been floating around in her head.

"You mean like *Saturday Night Live*?" Ben asked.

"Well, that's sketch comedy, which I like too. But I mean the kind where one person does a routine they wrote themselves."

"Like Sarah Silverman or Chris Rock," Ben said.

"Yeah, except they swear a lot, so I'm not allowed to watch them. My dad likes Jerry Seinfeld and Ellen DeGeneres because they work clean. I like them too, but actually my favorite comedians are Melissa McCarthy and Tina Fey, even though they mostly do movies and TV. But sometimes you have to start as a stand-up, and then when people know who you are, you get to do TV and movies." God, Izzy, you're blabbering, she said to herself.

Ben looked surprised. "I didn't know you were such an expert on comedy, Izzy."

"My dad wanted to *be* a comedian once. A long time ago. Before I was born."

"That's cool."

"Yeah. I kind of want . . ." She stopped herself. Was this information that she'd regret giving him?

"You want what? *You* want to be a comedian?"

She looked at him cautiously, biting her lip.

"That's awesome! Do you have a stand-up routine?"

She shook her head. "Not much of one. Not yet. I guess I've got the hair for it, though."

Ben's laugh was sharp. "I can see you being a comedian, Izzy. I really can. You have a way of saying things that's really funny."

"You think so?" Was that a compliment? From Ben?

Oliver leaned forward. "Tell him that joke about school, Izzy. The one you told me."

"I didn't *tell* you, Oliver. You were spying on me."

"Okay," Ben said. "Now you have to tell me."

Izzy blew out a big breath. "I'm not sure I remember it. Gimme a minute."

"It starts out, 'What's the deal with school,'" Oliver prompted.

"Okay, okay, I remember." Izzy got the joke in her mind and thought of how Jerry would deliver it, very coolly. "So, what's the deal with school?" Could she really do this in front of Ben Gustino? She took a deep breath.

"The first few years, sure: You learn to read, you count to a hundred, red and blue makes purple—that's good stuff. But after that, it's a big hassle! Every day you have to figure out what to wear so you'll be inconspicuous enough not to be called on in class, but not so invisible that nobody sits with you in the cafeteria. You gotta do well enough on the test that your parents don't freak out, but not so well that the teacher wants you to join the math team."

Ben and Oliver both laughed, and Izzy felt like a helium balloon let go to soar into the sky.

"Because if you think you're walking that tight-rope *now*—," she continued, a little giddy with her success, "you know, the one between 'I can almost see popularity from here' and 'maybe if I shaved my head someone would notice me'—once you become a mathlete, once you sign up for *mathletics*, you might as well just go eat lunch with the school librarian, because you are a complete social misfit."

Was that a good enough ending? Oliver was laughing, but what about Ben? She looked tentatively across the front seat.

Ben took his hands off the steering wheel long enough to clap. "Wow. I'm impressed, Izzy. You're funny! You thought that up yourself?"

"Well, sure. You can't use somebody else's material."

"I told you it was funny," Oliver said.

"What else you got?" Ben asked.

Izzy shrugged. "That's about it. It takes me a while to come up with funny stuff."

"Let's think of some more," Ben urged her. "There's lots that's funny about school, right? The teachers, gym class. The cafeteria alone is worth ten minutes."

Izzy stared out the window, and her mind started to click. When it sounded good in her head, she tried it out on her car audience. "Word travels fast around school when there's something edible for lunch. Like, 'Nachos today!' 'Yes! I love nachos!' But then you get up to the front of the line, and the lunch lady spoons up a big ladleful of . . . bright orange glue and dumps it over a bowl of crushed-up chips. That is not nachos! That's . . . cornflakes with squeeze cheese!"

Her audience laughed appreciatively.

"Squeeze cheese!" Oliver repeated, giggling.

"What about mystery meat?" Ben asked.

Izzy thought for a minute and then started, even though she wasn't sure where she was headed. "You can hide anything on a bun and call it a hamburger. The lunch ladies figure if it's shaped like a patty, we'll eat it. Could be stale doughnuts with a little ketchup on top, some old CDs they wanna get rid of . . ." *What else? You need at least three things. Move on. Keep the rhythm.* "You take a bite and *yum*, it tastes like old carpeting you just wiped your boots on . . . And don't you love a good veggie burger? There can be *anything* inside that hockey puck: turnips, Brussels sprouts . . . whatever was left over from yesterday's salad bar—a rose bush is a vegetable, right? It's *all natural!*"

"Yeah!" Ben cried. "Izzy's on a roll."

"A hamburger roll!" Oliver added.

"Mashed potatoes!" Izzy announced. "They take an ice-cream scoop, which gets your hopes up. You think something really tasty is about to plop on your wet, hot plastic tray—which has apparently just been to a sauna—and then *splooch!* That is definitely *not* ice cream. Looks kinda like . . . a wad of soggy toilet paper with a tablespoon of compost mixed in for flavor." They giggled again, and Izzy felt unstoppable.

"And then there's always fruit," she continued. *Fruit? What about fruit?* "They give you a choice. You can have an apple left over from . . ." *From what?*

"From the War of 1812!" Ben said.

"Right!" Izzy said. "And if you don't want the apple, you can have a banana that won't be ripe . . ."

"'Until the next century!" Oliver shouted. He was so pleased with himself that he fell over sideways and clunked his head on the window, but he kept laughing anyway. Izzy hadn't seen him laugh so hard since the night he and Ben watched *Monty Python*. Only this time, *she* had made it happen. And this time they were all laughing together, which felt so good that, for a moment, Izzy wished their trip never had to end.

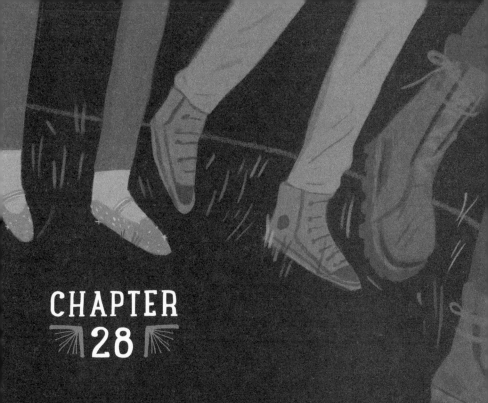

CHAPTER 28

Their big breakfast held them for a long time, but around one o'clock Ben pulled the car over, and they passed around the apples and the peanut-butter jar. The hilarity of the morning had tapered off and left them feeling comfortable and tired. Soon after they got back on the road, Oliver fell asleep in the back seat.

Izzy tried to make sense of Ben's map and directions. "How much farther, do you think?" she asked.

"Couple hours. We're almost past the Finger Lakes."

"I didn't see any lakes."

"We're south of them." He yawned and swiveled his head around on his neck.

"Are you sleepy?" Izzy asked him.

"A little. Rough night last night."

"Yeah." They hadn't discussed what had happened the night before, and Izzy was starting to wonder if they ever would. She could feel her heart speed up as she remembered their middle-of-the-night breakdown. Even if they never talked about it, she was sure none of them would ever forget it.

"Talk to me," Ben said. "That'll keep me awake."

"Okay. Do you think we'll find Uncle Henderson? I mean, will he be there at the lake?"

Ben sighed. "God, I hope so."

"Me too. But what if he isn't?"

"I guess we'll figure that out when we need to."

"If he's not there, I think we should call our parents anyway. My mom must be really worried by now." She wondered if her dad even knew she was gone. Was he worried too, or didn't he care?

Ben nodded, but he didn't look at her.

"Your dad's probably upset too," she said.

"I don't want to talk about my dad, okay?" His grip tightened on the steering wheel and he sped up a little bit.

"Okay," she agreed.

A few minutes passed in silence until Ben took

his eyes off the road for a second and looked over at Izzy. "Still like your shoes?"

"I love them," she said. "Thanks. Thanks a lot." It turned out, the more you said that word, the easier it got.

"You're welcome."

And then, for no reason at all, she said, "My dad and his new wife are having a baby. A boy. I just found out."

Ben made a whistling noise. "That's a big deal, huh?"

She shrugged. "I guess."

"Sounds like you're not too thrilled about it."

"Why should I be? It's just another excuse for my dad to ignore me."

"Well, at least you'll have a brother."

Izzy sighed. "Big deal."

"Well, maybe *you* don't care, but the new kid might."

Izzy hadn't thought of that. "Maybe, but he won't care for a while. He'll just be a baby at first."

"That's true. And people make such a big fuss about babies."

Izzy could just imagine it. Even if she did get to see her father once in a while, the new baby would probably be with them every minute. He wouldn't be able to talk to her because he'd be too busy spooning pureed prunes into its dribbly mouth or changing its disgusting diapers. He'd be talking baby talk and smelling its head in that stupid way adults always did. She might as well not even have a father.

But as soon as that thought floated into her brain, she pushed it out again. It wasn't true. She *did* have a father, even if he ignored her. It was Oliver who didn't have a mother anymore, who didn't even know where his father *was*, and that, she reminded herself, was infinitely worse.

"Hey." Ben reached over and swatted her shoulder. She looked up.

"What?"

"Too bad the baby's a boy, huh?"

"What do you mean?"

"You probably wanted a sister. I mean, you've already *got* two brothers."

Izzy was so surprised, she was speechless. Ben gave her a genuine smile—the second one in less than twenty-four hours. It was possible she'd never felt better in her life.

CHAPTER
🎇 29 🎇

Izzy was just drifting off to sleep, her head resting against the window, when she heard Oliver say, "Ben, how come *your* mother left?" She kept her eyes closed and listened—this was information she was interested in.

Ben tried to get off easy. "You know, divorce. It happens."

But Oliver wasn't buying it. "Usually when people get divorced, the kids go back and forth, or they live with their mother. I never heard of anybody just living with their father."

"Well, I guess I'm different." His voice sounded tight in his throat.

Oliver wouldn't let it go. "But, you *could* go live with your mother if you wanted to, right?"

There was a long pause before Ben said, "No, Oliver, I can't. My mother moved to California so she could be as far away as possible from her crappy husband." He hesitated for a minute and then added, "And her crappy kid."

Izzy was fully awake now.

"What do you mean?" Oliver pressed.

Ben grunted, and the car picked up speed. "I mean, she left because of me. She couldn't stand being around me anymore." His voice was getting louder and louder. "She said my dad and I were as boring as two weeks of steady rain, and she was sick and tired of being a wife and mother. She moved to the other side of the country to get away from us. I chased her away, Oliver. It was my fault she left, so no, I can't go live with her."

Izzy sat up, her mouth gaping. "She said that to you?" Izzy had never heard of a parent saying such an awful thing. Sure, her father ignored her, but he wasn't mean to her.

"She said it to my dad, but I heard her," Ben said. "The whole neighborhood heard her."

Suddenly the trees seemed to be racing past

the car. Izzy sneaked a look at the speedometer. "Um, Ben, I think you should slow down."

He looked where she was looking. "Sorry. I didn't realize . . ." The car slowed to the speed limit.

Oliver's voice from the back seat was quiet, but Izzy could hear anger rising into it. "That's not what you told me before."

"What do you mean? I didn't tell you anything before."

"Yes, you did. You told me it wasn't my fault what happened to my mother. You said a kid can't make an adult do something like that. But now you said it's your fault *your* mother moved away. So, that's the same thing!"

Ben didn't answer for a minute. Izzy kept her eyes fixed on him, watching his Adam's apple bob up and down.

"It's not the same thing at all," he said finally. "Your mother had an actual illness—mine was just sick of me."

"It *is* the same," Oliver insisted, his face blotchy with anger. "My mother wanted to get away from Dad and me just like your mom did. She just did it a different way. If it was your fault, then it was *my* fault too."

For a second the car wobbled in and out of its lane. Ben put on the turn signal and looked for a place to pull over. "Oliver," he said, "if your mom had only wanted to get away from you, she would have moved, like mine did. It must have been worse than that for her. She wanted to get away . . . from herself."

"Stop lying to me!" Oliver yelled. "Now I wish I didn't give myself this tattoo!"

"*What* tattoo?" Izzy yelled.

Ben pulled the car over and turned it off. He and Izzy unbuckled their seat belts and turned around to see Oliver peel off his sweatshirt. As he threw it aside, they saw on his arm a smeary red drawing of a bird, its big wings spread all over his small bicep.

"I drew it this morning before you guys woke up," he said. "It was supposed to be a phoenix, like Ben's. Uncle Steve said it means you can start over and have a new life, but that's not true. You only get one life, and if you screw it up, you don't get another chance." He flopped over on his side, his scribbled-on arm across his face.

Izzy didn't know what to say. "Is that marker? Where'd you get a red marker?"

"I took it from Ellis's office," he mumbled. "Because *I'm* a crappy kid too."

"You are not. Ben, tell him!"

Ben had been running his hand through his hair, and it was standing up funny now. "God,

Oliver, you're not a bad kid for taking a stupid marker. Ellis probably would have given it to you anyway. Don't be a bonehead."

"*You're* a bonehead," Oliver spat back.

"Okay, I'm a bonehead too. But listen, you're right about the phoenix. The reason I got that tattoo was so I'd be reminded that I could start over, that my life could get better."

"You're a bonehead phoenix," Oliver mumbled.

"Oliver, I'm trying to start over, but it's hard. I don't even know who I want to be! And maybe you have to start over now too, but that doesn't mean we're alike in every way." Ben reached between the seats and put his hand on Oliver's shoulder. "I'm *absolutely sure* it wasn't your fault your mother killed herself."

Izzy and Oliver both flinched. Nobody ever said it out loud like that, and the words hung in the air like skywriting.

And then Izzy saw what the actual truth just might be. "Maybe you are alike," she said. "I mean, I don't think it's your fault either, Ben." His head bobbed back, and he looked at her sideways, as if he weren't sure he wanted to hear her opinion.

But Izzy was pretty sure she was right about this. "It's not Oliver's fault his mother . . . killed herself. And I doubt that it's your fault your mother moved to California. I mean, I don't know why she left, but Ben, how could *you* be boring? Maybe being a mother was boring, and okay, your dad's kind of boring, but not you. Parents do what they want, not what we make them do. They're the *grown-ups*."

Ben looked at her with narrowed eyes, and Izzy couldn't tell what was going on behind them. After a second he said, "So, you think my dad's boring?"

She shrugged. "He can't help it. He's a dentist."

A burst of laughter escaped Ben's throat. "You're something, Izzy. You really are."

It wasn't exactly a compliment, but Izzy felt good about it anyway. Besides which, making Ben Gustino laugh felt like a superpower.

Ben glanced back at Oliver. "We're almost there, dude. Let's just finish the trip, okay? We'll talk about this later. In fact, once we find your dad and get back home, we can talk about it as much as you want for as long as you want."

Oliver didn't respond. He was sitting up now, spitting on his "tattoo" and rubbing at it with the palm of his hand until it was a rusty-looking mess. Ben started up the car and got back on the road. Nobody said a word for half an hour, until Ben pointed out the window and said, "That's it. Lake Chautauqua."

"We're here!" Izzy shouted, even though the blue water was barely visible in the distance.

"How do we get close to it?" Oliver was obviously trying to keep the excitement out of his voice, but Izzy could hear it pushing through.

She shuffled through Ben's maps. "It looks like this road eventually runs right up next to it."

The three of them stared silently at Lake Chautauqua for several minutes until Oliver said what they were probably all thinking. "It's a big lake."

"Yeah," Ben said. "Do you remember where the trailer is? When were you here last?"

"I don't know. Maybe a year ago. Maybe two." His voice was quiet and a little squeaky. "My mom was with us that time."

Izzy turned around in her seat. "She was?"

Oliver nodded. "She used to come here with Dad a lot before I was born. He'd write songs while she walked in the woods."

"By herself?"

"Yeah. Sometimes she saw bears, but she wasn't afraid of them. She thought they were beautiful."

"I wish—" Izzy began, and then stopped. Should she say that? Would it hurt Oliver or make him feel better? It was hard to know, but sometimes you had to say what you meant. "I wish I'd spent more time getting to know your mom. She was always so quiet when you came to visit. I should have talked to her more."

Oliver didn't say anything, but he didn't look any sadder than usual. Or maybe that wasn't possible.

"There's a tourist information booth," Ben said. "Let's stop and see if we can get a better map."

The booth was closed, but there was a map posted in a glass case on an outside wall. On the map, a dozen or more small towns lined both sides of the lake.

"Do any of these places sound familiar?" Ben asked Oliver. "Greenhurst? Belleview? Sherman's Bay?"

Oliver shook his head and kept studying the map as his eyes welled up. His hands were balled into fists. "I didn't think it would be so big," he said.

Izzy felt frustration building in her chest. What had made them believe they were going to be able to find a tiny old trailer hidden on an enormous lake? "Oliver, *think*," she said. "You must remember something!"

Ben gave her a grim look, and she managed to clamp her mouth shut. Oliver was doing the best he could.

"You said the trailer was in a wooded area. Was it right on the lake?" Ben asked.

Oliver wiped away an escaped tear. "Not right on it, but not too far. You could walk to the lake."

Suddenly his eyes widened. "What does that say, that town up at the top?"

"This one? Dewittville."

"That might be it. Yeah, we got groceries there. I remember that name!" There was a light in Oliver's eyes.

"Okay, back in the car," Ben said. He checked the route on his phone and announced, "We're twenty minutes away."

Twenty minutes that seemed like hours. Oliver sat forward, clutching the back of Izzy's seat and peering determinedly out the window. She could hardly bear the wait herself. They were so close to finding Uncle Henderson. If he was here. If he hadn't . . . done something awful. If I feel this sick to my stomach, she thought, what does Oliver feel like?

The sun was just starting to sink in the sky when Oliver shouted, "There! Thumb Road! I remember the name because it was so weird! That's it!"

Ben slowed the car. "Should I turn here?"

"Yes! Yes!" Oliver bounced on the seat as Ben turned the corner. "It's not far now. You turn off on a dirt road that you almost can't see. It goes down a little hill into the trees. Right there!"

Ben had passed the road, but he turned the car around and went back. "Here? This doesn't even look drivable."

"I know! That's why nobody ever finds him! But *we* did. We found him!" Oliver pasted himself to the window, the better to get the first glimpse of his father.

As the Malibu bumped along the rutted road, Izzy hoped Oliver was right. After all they'd been through the past two days, it would be terrible if Uncle Henderson weren't here.

"How far?" Ben asked. Izzy could tell he was excited too. His eyebrows had lifted up almost into his hair, and he drummed his hands on the steering wheel.

"It should be right . . . there!" Oliver said.

And sure enough, a rusty hulk of a trailer was parked under a canopy of golden leaves, and sitting out front on a plastic patio chair was Henderson Hook, holding his guitar against his chest like a shield.

CHAPTER 30

The car hadn't come to a full stop before Oliver bolted out. "Dad!" he screamed. "Dad!"

Izzy watched as Uncle Henderson looked up from his music, his eyes cloudy and far away. He didn't have time to put down the guitar before Oliver leaped on him, knocking it sideways so it hung off his shoulder. Oliver threw his arms around his father, and finally Uncle Henderson hugged him back. Izzy felt proud of Oliver, though she wasn't sure why. Maybe because he hadn't given up. He'd known where his father would be, and he'd led them right to him.

But on the outskirts of her happiness, Izzy could feel the sharp edges of anger. She remembered the scream that had risen from her cousin's chest the night before, his howl of fear and loneliness. This search had almost been too much for him, and there was a part of Izzy that felt like cracking her uncle's precious guitar in half and throwing it in the lake. And maybe even pushing him in after it.

"We found you!" Oliver said, clinging to his father like a vine to a tree.

"I guess you did," Uncle Henderson said. Izzy was glad to hear her uncle speak, even though his voice sounded as if it had been pulled back into his body from far away. He looked over at Ben and Izzy standing by the car as if he couldn't quite place them.

"Why did you leave without telling me?" Oliver was on his knees on Uncle Henderson's lap, his arms still around his father's neck. He sat back and looked him right in the eyes. "I was scared, Dad. I thought you weren't coming back!"

"Don't I always come back?" Uncle Henderson said. It sounded to Izzy as if he were asking himself the question.

"But it's different now." Oliver shook his head, struggling to explain the problem. "Dad, you can't do this anymore!"

Uncle Henderson smiled his faraway smile and

lifted Oliver off his lap. "I wasn't expecting company today," he said. "I started a new song this morning, and I'm just figuring out the melody line." He began to arrange the guitar in front of him again, in the slow, sleepy way he'd done everything the past couple of months.

In three long strides Ben was on top of Uncle Henderson. His jaws pulsed with anger as he grabbed the guitar and pulled it away from him. "What the hell is wrong with you, man?" he yelled in Uncle Henderson's face. "You've got a kid to take care of, a kid who doesn't have a mother anymore. You can't just think about yourself! You can't just walk off and disappear! You scared the crap out of him. He thought you were *dead*!"

Izzy was shocked to see her uncle's face slowly crumble. "Maybe I *am* dead," he said. "I'm the living dead."

And then Oliver was suddenly angry too. "No, you're not! You're not dead!" His small fists pummeled his father's arm and shoulder and back until finally Uncle Henderson got up out of the chair and held Oliver's arms to stop the punching.

"I'm sorry, Oliver," he said. "I know I'm a lousy father. That's why I left you with Aunt Maggie. She's stronger than I am. She can take care of you."

"I don't want her to take care of me," Oliver yelled. "I want *you* to!"

Izzy walked closer. "It's your job, Uncle Hen. Oliver needs you."

Uncle Henderson shook his head. "He doesn't need me. You've been a good friend to him, Izzy. You and the boy here. I think it's better for Oliver if I'm not around so much—"

"No, it's not!" Izzy felt like slapping him. "That's the dumbest thing you've ever said, Uncle Hen."

Oliver wrapped himself around his father's leg as tears puddled in the hollows beneath Uncle Henderson's eyes.

"You don't understand," Uncle Henderson said. "I can't do it without her. I can't—"

"Of course you can do it!" Ben said. He grabbed Uncle Henderson's upper arm in a tight grip. "You're the adult. You're the father. You *have* to do it. Just *do it*, dude."

A spark seemed to light behind Uncle Henderson's eyes, and suddenly his furious face was inches away from Ben's. He roared, "*I can't*! You're a kid— you don't know what you're talking about. I'm not strong enough! *I cannot do it*!" He kicked the lawn chair aside and strode off toward the woods, walking fast, as if he were actually headed somewhere.

But Oliver was not about to watch his father disappear again. "No," he screamed, tears beginning to fall. "Don't leave me again, Daddy! Don't leave me!"

Uncle Henderson took another step or two, then stopped and turned around. For a minute he locked eyes with his son, and both were motionless. Then, slowly, he held out his hand. Oliver ran to him and grabbed it, and the two of them walked into the darkening woods together.

CHAPTER 31

Izzy turned on Ben's phone and made the first call. "Mom? It's me. We found Uncle Hen."

"Izzy! My God, where are you? I drove all over the state of . . . where *are* you?"

Izzy sighed. She was going to pay for this for a long time. "I'm sorry, Mom. We're in New York at Lake Chautauqua. Where are you?"

"I'm home. I came back to get Michael. Why are you at some lake? Is Oliver with you? And Ben? What is going on?"

Izzy explained that Ben had driven the "bor-rowed" car carefully on the back roads, that Oliver knew just where to find his father, and that Uncle Hen had gone to his hidden trailer to write music. She didn't tell her mother about car trouble or ground hornets or nightmares. She didn't tell her about late-night haircuts, or breakfast with Ellis, or phoenix tattoos. She didn't tell her that Uncle Henderson and Oliver had walked off into the woods together. There were so many stories that she would probably tell her mother eventually, but for now she wanted to keep some things just among the three of them.

"Ben bought me socks and sneakers at a Goodwill for seven dollars," she said. She would tell her mother that much, even though her mother was not likely to understand what a great thing it was to have shoes, finally, that fit, and to have them because Ben hurt when she hurt.

"Oh, Izzy, sometimes you make me so mad," her mother said. "I can't believe the three of you drove all the way across New York State! What if you'd been pulled over by the police? What if Henderson hadn't been there? And you hitchhiked! When I think of what might have happened to you, it makes me weak in the knees. You can never scare me like this again, do you understand? You're all I've got, Izzy!"

"No, I'm not. What about Dr. Gustino? And Uncle Hen? And Oliver?"

"It's not the same." Her mother's voice softened. "You're my child, Izzy. You're more important to me than anyone else."

Which Izzy was glad to hear, though she knew her mother would still punish her even if she was more important than anyone else. "I'm sorry, Mom. I really am. But we didn't know what else to do. Oliver was so scared—he needed to find his dad. And you weren't doing anything about it, so Ben and I did."

"Izzy, you and Ben are not grown-ups. It's not your place to take care of Oliver. I know you meant well, but—"

"Just because you're a grown-up doesn't mean you're always right." It was kind of a mean thing to say, but it was the truth.

Her mother was silent for a long time. Izzy could hear her clearing her throat. Finally she said, "Sweetheart, I do the best I can. We'll discuss this later. Let me talk to Henderson now."

Uh-oh. "Um, he and Oliver went into the woods to . . . get some branches to make a fire. I'll tell him to call you as soon as they get back, okay?"

Reluctantly, her mother agreed. "You can tell Ben I'm calling Michael this minute."

Ben took his phone back and waited. Not two minutes passed before it buzzed angrily. From what Izzy could tell, Ben's conversation with his father was quite a bit worse than the one she'd had with her mother. Ben said almost nothing. In fact his clenched jaws seemed determined not to let any sound escape at all. Izzy was pretty sure Dr. Gustino was not telling Ben he was more important than anyone else.

"They're leaving Coolidge now," Ben reported after he hung up. "They're coming in your mom's car so my dad can drive Uncle Steve's car back. They'll stop somewhere overnight and be here before noon tomorrow."

"Is he really mad?" Izzy asked.

"What do you think?" Ben flopped into the lawn chair and leaned forward, the palms of his hands holding up his head. "I'm grounded until after Christmas, I'm only allowed to use my computer for homework, and I'm not allowed to see Uncle Steve again. Ever."

"That's not fair!" Izzy said. "It wasn't your uncle's fault!"

Ben choked out a laugh. "You didn't like him at first, Izzy. You thought he was some kind of deviant. Admit it."

She blushed. "Well, Oliver told me about the beer and the pot. And he's got that big beard and everything."

"Yeah, facial hair is terrifying." Ben was teasing her, but at least the scowl had lifted off his face. He picked up Uncle Henderson's guitar and strummed it idly.

Izzy saw them first as they reappeared from the stand of trees, silently checking their surroundings like cautious woodland animals. Uncle Henderson looked right at her, his head sitting solidly on his shoulders. "Uncle Hen!" she cried.

Oliver still held tight to his father's hand, but he looked calmer than he had when they left. "It's getting dark," Uncle Henderson said. "How long are you guys gonna sit outside?"

"We were waiting for you," Izzy said.

Ben put down the guitar and stood up. "I shouldn't have talked to you that way," he said. "I'm sorry."

"Don't be sorry," Uncle Henderson said. He brushed a sleeve over his face, and Izzy could see the gleam of tears in the fading light. His lips curled into something resembling a weak smile. "You were right. It was time I heard it."

"We talked," Oliver said as he looked up into his father's face. "Dad's talking again. He's gonna come home."

Uncle Henderson nodded. "I'm gonna try my best, for Oliver's sake."

o o o o o o o o o o o o

It sounded to Izzy as if her mother were giving Uncle Henderson a lecture, but he was speaking to her in full sentences, which seemed like a step in the right direction.

"They've got sleeping bags with them," Uncle Hen said calmly. "There's enough room for everybody in the trailer for one night. They made it this far, Mags—they'll be fine until you get here." He listened to his older sister for another long minute and then said, "I know, Maggie. I'm sorry I scared everybody. I get it. I do."

Izzy was curled up on a corner of the musty futon that served as Uncle Henderson's bed and couch, a heavy feeling in her chest that she recognized as sadness. It seemed like she and Ben and Oliver had been on this journey together for weeks instead of only days. So much had happened, but tomorrow their adventure would be over and they'd be separated, Ben going home with his furious father, and she, Oliver, and Uncle Hen with her mother. The scoldings would be rough, and Ben would no doubt get it worse than she would, because he was the oldest, and the driver, and because he'd gotten in trouble before. Izzy wished she could ride with him so he didn't have to face his father all alone.

Why couldn't Dr. Gustino see how responsible Ben had been? Maybe he did a few things he

wasn't supposed to do, but he also took care of
Oliver when the grown-ups weren't. And he took
care of her too, buying her shoes and fixing her
stupid hair. They should be *thanking* Ben, not
punishing him.

It seemed to Izzy that she was a different person
now than she'd been the night they sneaked away
from her house and hitchhiked to Eastman with
the red-headed truck driver. She didn't want
Uncle Henderson and Oliver to go back to Wilton
anymore. And she didn't want to go back to *her*
old life either, the one where she rattled around in
that big old house with only her mother for company. She wished Ben could come back to their
house and live in the basement again. She and
Oliver could hang out down there with him and
watch Monty Python, and he could help her with
her comedy routine. But all that, she knew, would
not happen.

Uncle Henderson, who hadn't seemed able to
do much more than open a bottle of beer for the
past few months, heated up a can of soup and got
out a pan to make them grilled cheese sandwiches.
He noticed the marker mess on Oliver's arm and
made him clean it off with soap and water instead
of just spit. When the soup was hot, he poured it
into the only three mugs in the trailer and handed
one to each of them.

"I'll eat when you're finished," he said, just like a normal parent might. Oliver sat on his father's lap while he slurped up the soup, and Uncle Henderson kept an arm around his waist. "It's good to see you," he said to his son, brushing the hair back off Oliver's forehead. "I'm glad you came."

"Me too," Oliver said, leaning into his father's chest. "I like it here."

"Next time we'll come out together. We'll go fishing."

Oliver beamed. "Can Ben come too? And Izzy?"

"Sure," Uncle Henderson said. "We'll have a fishing party."

Izzy was going to make sure that he kept that promise.

When they finished eating, there was a pleasant silence in the room, as if they were all happy to be where they were—here, in the middle of nowhere, one more night together before all hell broke loose. Ben collected the plates and mugs and put them in the sink. "Henderson," he said, "do you think you could teach me to play the guitar sometime?"

"Sure," Uncle Hen said. "I'll give you a lesson now, soon as I wash up the dishes."

"I'll do the dishes," Izzy said, jumping up. "I like to listen to you play."

"Can you teach me that song you wrote, the one

you sometimes play at night?" Ben asked. "The one that goes, 'It's not a weakness if your heart breaks—'"

"Just a little!" Oliver finished the line.

Uncle Henderson's face paled, and for a moment it seemed as if the lights in his eyes had gone out again, but then he sat up straight and nodded at Ben. "That's a pretty good song, isn't it? Hand me my guitar, Oliver."

And that's how they spent the rest of the evening in the old trailer—Uncle Henderson teaching Ben the chords to his favorite songs, and Oliver and Izzy singing along. They sang "Be Always Tender" over and over, all four of them together, their voices getting stronger every time.

CHAPTER
32

As Izzy's mother's car crossed New York State, heading for home, Uncle Henderson sat in the back seat with Oliver, his arm firmly around his son, watching him sleep.

The front seat was silent at first too. The rain came down steadily, and Izzy's mother stared out the window through the wiper blades. She and Dr. Gustino had both exploded at their children the minute they walked into the trailer, and now she seemed exhausted. Izzy was still thinking about her mother's lecture about the dangers of hitchhiking (which had kind of terrified her) and imagining what it would be like to be grounded for a month (which she knew could have been an even longer sentence).

The Malibu had left the lake first, Ben and his father both silently furious. Oliver had given Ben a hug, and Izzy had waved as he got into the car, but there was nothing either of them could do to make his drive home any easier.

They weren't more than ten miles down the road when her mother said, "Get the phone out of my purse and call your father, Izzy. I told him you would."

"Does *he* know about this?" Izzy rummaged through the purse at her feet and pulled out the smartphone in the plain black case.

"Of course he does. He's your father. I've talked to him half a dozen times in the past two days."

Huh. That must be more than she'd talked to him in the past two years. Izzy placed the call, wondering what on earth she'd say to her father, or what he'd say to her.

"Izzy, is that you?" His voice sounded rough, like his vocal cords had been sandpapered.

"It's me."

"Are you okay?"

"Yeah, I'm fine. All I did was ride in a car for a couple of days."

"Well, your mother was very worried. And so

was I. And so was Emily. You can't just take off like that without telling anybody where you're going."

"I left a note," Izzy said. She tried to imagine her father and Emily sitting around their beautiful condo worrying about her. What would that even look like?

"Well, not a very instructive note," he grumbled.

"I'm sorry Mom called you. I didn't think she would."

For a moment he was silent. "Why wouldn't she call me?" he said finally. "I'm your *father*."

"I know, but . . . you're not my father the way you used to be," she said, her voice just barely above a whisper.

Suddenly he was yelling. "I can't believe you think that, Izzy! Just because I don't live with you now doesn't mean . . . I'm still your father!"

"Okay," she said, sorry now that she'd brought it up.

"It's *not* okay. I feel terrible that you think that."

He sighed deeply, and for a moment neither of them said anything. When he spoke again, his voice had changed, softened. "Maybe this is all my fault."

"What's your fault?"

"Everything. You ruining your hair and running off with Oliver and that teenage boy."

"It didn't have anything to do with you. Ben and I wanted to help Oliver."

"Your mother said you hitchhiked."

"Only once."

"Well, that's one time too many!"

"I *know*. Mom already gave me a big lecture about it."

"Your mother also said you've been upset about the new baby. Is that what's behind all this?"

God, when had the two of them gotten so chatty?

"I should have known that would be hard for you, Izzy. Sometimes I'm kind of stupid about things like that, you know?" She didn't answer him.

He sighed again. "Anyway, I'm glad that you're safe, and that Henderson is coming home. I hope we can . . . talk more. Emily and I would like you to be part of your brother's life. We really want that. Okay?"

"Yeah, I guess so." Why did he always have to say "we"? "Emily and I" was not her father.

There was an awkward silence for a moment, but then her father broke it. "Oh, by the way, I wanted to tell you—guess who we saw last weekend? Live and in person! Jerry Seinfeld!"

Izzy tried to keep the excitement out of her voice, but it was hard. "You did? You always wanted to see him!"

"You can imagine how thrilled I was. It was a last-minute thing. One of Emily's friends had tickets, but she couldn't go, so she gave them to us. I wish you could have come with us. You still like him, don't you? When he tours here again, I'm going to take you. That's a promise!"

Jerry Seinfeld, in person! "Was he great? Did you fall out of your chair laughing?"

"I did, Izzy. He was *so* funny."

"Dad, you know what?" She was just going to tell him, even if he didn't care. "I'm making up a comedy routine. You know, stand-up."

"Really?" He sounded excited. "You didn't tell me you were doing that! Wow, Izzy, I can't wait to see what you've got! Maybe you can come for a visit before the baby arrives. We could watch some of our favorite old CDs—early *SNL* from the Gilda Radner days! We haven't done that in so long."

"Could we rent the new Melissa McCarthy movie too?" she dared to ask. "I haven't seen it yet."

"Great idea! Let's do that!"

"Okay." And then, so he wouldn't hear that her voice had suddenly gotten all waterlogged like some weepy little kid, she said, "I have to go now. I'll talk to you later." She turned her face to the window and pretended to look out at the soggy scenery, but she kept the phone cradled in her lap as if all the best moments of her childhood lived inside it.

CHAPTER 33

It hadn't occurred to Izzy that going missing for a few days would make her an instant celebrity at Coolidge Middle School. Cookie and Pauline were waiting for her out front when her mother dropped her off. Apparently they'd reinstated Izzy as a best friend during her absence, and as such they felt it was their right to be the first to pounce on her. Within seconds a dozen other girls surrounded her too, all of them eager to hear about her experiences as a runaway.

"What happened to you?" Cookie asked. "We were so worried about you, Izzy!"

"Oh, your hair!" Pauline said. "You fixed it! It looks good now."

"Ben cut it for me," Izzy said, trying to sound nonchalant.

A murmur went through the crowd of girls. Cookie's mouth fell open, and Pauline put out her hand to touch Izzy's cropped hair, as if feeling it with her own fingers would help her to believe the unbelievable.

"He did not!" Cookie said.

Izzy shrugged. "His mom was a hairdresser. She taught him how."

"But we heard Ben kidnapped you and made you drive to Pennsylvania!" Pauline said, crinkling up her eyes.

"That's the silliest thing I ever heard," Izzy said. "Nobody kidnapped anybody. We *wanted* to go. And it wasn't Pennsylvania—only New York."

"But why would you run away with *him*?" Cookie wanted to know.

"We weren't running away. We went to find my uncle." Izzy had a feeling she was never going to be able to explain the trip to her friends. They'd never be able to understand the journey she and Oliver and Ben had been on, because neither of them had ever felt so desperate. They'd never lost anyone. They'd never felt hope leak out of a hole in their hearts. Suddenly they seemed so young, and Izzy wondered if maybe she'd out-grown *them*.

"I heard Ben Gustino stole a car," Cookie announced to the gathering crowd. "Somebody said he robbed a man in Eastman!"

Izzy was getting more than a little annoyed by these exaggerations. "Ben's uncle lives in East-man, and we borrowed his car." Okay, that wasn't entirely true either, but it was the story she was sticking to.

Comments flew wildly around Izzy's head. "I heard they hitchhiked to New York." "That Ben kid isn't old enough to drive." "My brother said they had an accident." The circle closed in on Izzy more and more by the minute. This was not the way she wanted to be the center of attention.

"I heard Ben Gustino is on drugs," one girl said, and a murmur of agreement went through the crowd.

Izzy whirled around and glared at her. "That's a horrible lie!" Izzy yelled. "You're spreading rumors about somebody you don't even know!"

The circle of girls hushed and stared at Izzy, shocked. She grabbed Cookie's and Pauline's arms and pulled them away from the larger group and around the side of the brick building. "I don't want to talk about this in front of everybody," she said. "They've got it all wrong."

"But, Izzy, you must have been scared, weren't you?" Pauline asked. "You were gone for almost three whole days with *Ben Gustino*!"

"God, Pauline, he's not Dracula. He's not who you think he is at all. He's really . . . nice. More than nice. He . . . he bought me these shoes." All three of them gazed down at the gray and pink sneakers. Just thinking about the shoes made Izzy's throat hurt. Had she thanked Ben enough? Not just for the shoes—for everything. Did he know how sorry she was for being so hard on him at first? Sorry for being just as dumb as all these other girls who pretended to know who he was, when all they really knew was gossip and rumors. Ben was in so much trouble for doing such a good thing. She hoped he knew how much she appreciated it.

Cookie and Pauline glanced at her sneakers, confused. They had sad-puppy looks on their faces, as if they thought she'd been brainwashed by aliens.

"Why did he buy you shoes?" Pauline asked quietly, as if she were a little afraid to hear the answer.

"I don't want to talk about it anymore," Izzy said. "You guys don't get it." She started to walk away, but Cookie caught her arm and dragged her back.

"We're *trying* to get it, Izzy. We really are. Do you, like, have a crush on Ben or something?"

Izzy sighed. "Oh, Cookie, *no*." She should have known that would be the way Cookie would see it. How could she explain to them that there were other ways to be close to people, ways that could be even more important than holding hands in the hallway or giggling together in study hall? "Ben took care of us, Oliver and me. And we tried to take care of him too."

Cookie and Pauline exchanged puzzled looks. This was not the conversation they had expected to have with Izzy this morning, and they were stumped.

Finally Pauline said, "Well, at least you're home now, and everything can go back to normal."

Izzy nodded, but she couldn't make herself smile. "Back to normal" was not where she wanted to be anymore.

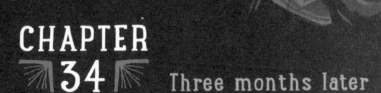

CHAPTER 34

Three months later

Tonight would be the first time Uncle Henderson was back onstage in six months, since the night he'd come home from his gig to find Aunt Felicia dead. He would have put off performing for longer, but when Patsy Kennedy had had to cancel her December concert at the Bellwood Theater with only a week's notice, the booking agent had called his friend Fred Dumont. Fred had told him Henderson Hook was living right there in Coolidge these days and was back on his feet, ready to play. Which was not entirely true, but Uncle Henderson had taken a deep breath and agreed to do it.

When Izzy came downstairs, dressed for the concert in stylish new boots—an early and surprising Christmas present from her mother— Uncle Henderson did not look at all "back on his feet." He was sitting in a corner of the parlor in the dark, trembling.

"Uncle Hen, I thought you were supposed to be at the theater by now," Izzy said. "Where's Mom?"

"She's getting my anxiety pills to calm me down," he said. "But I don't think I can do it. It's too soon."

"But Uncle Hen, there are so many people who want to hear you play again. You can't let them down!" As soon as the words were out of her mouth, Izzy thought maybe that wasn't the right thing to say. Uncle Henderson looked more frightened than ever, and she was afraid he was imagining all those people in the audience staring at him.

Izzy's mother came down the stairs with a pill in her hand and a glass of water. "Take this," she said to her brother. "Then close your eyes and just breathe for a minute. Izzy, let's get out of here and let Hen try to relax."

It was a long way, Izzy thought, from the place Uncle Henderson was now to relaxation. "Where's Oliver?" she asked as she followed her mother to the kitchen.

"He's in the basement, getting ready," her mom said. Once Ben had moved back home, Oliver had asked to live in the basement. Izzy thought it was a good sign that he was willing to be a little farther away from his father these days, and also that he obviously wanted to be just like Ben (no tattoos, though). No one talked about Uncle Henderson and Oliver moving back to Wilton anymore, and Izzy hoped they never would.

"We should call Ben," Izzy said. "He knows how to talk to Uncle Hen. He'll get him to play tonight." Izzy's house, school, and his own house were the only places Ben had been allowed to go all fall. He was taking guitar lessons from Uncle Henderson now, and the two had gotten to be good friends.

"Not a bad idea," her mother said. "Ben is kind of a miracle worker with Henderson. The kid should be a therapist when he grows up."

Izzy made a face. "No, he should be a song-writer. They help way more people than therapists do." Her mother laughed, but Izzy wasn't kidding.

Her mother called Michael. They were all planning to go to the concert together anyway, but her mom said, "Come over now. We need Ben."

Izzy had been trying to get comfortable calling Dr. Gustino by his first name. Her mother had been dating him for seven months, which was a record for her, and one night Izzy had overheard them talking about "taking the next step." Izzy didn't really mind Dr. Gustino anymore, but she was still shocked at the idea that he could become a permanent fixture in her life. On the other hand, she also immediately saw what the upside to the situation was, and it more than made up for her discomfort with the dentist. If Michael was going to end up being her stepfather, Ben would *really* be her brother, and that would be the best change ever.

Ben came in with his guitar over his shoulder and went into the dim parlor, patting Izzy's shoulder as he passed by. Oliver had come up from the basement by then, and the two of them stood in the doorway, watching anxiously.

Whatever Ben said to Uncle Henderson, he said it quietly. All Izzy could hear was her mother fretting to Michael about how Uncle Henderson was going to miss his sound check. Ben absent-mindedly strummed his own guitar. He seemed to be asking Uncle Henderson a question. Sure enough, before long Hen picked up his instrument and started to play. The two of them sang a quiet duet. Little by little Uncle Henderson sat up straighter, his voice deepening into its signature rumble.

In a few minutes they were all on their feet and hurrying outside to the two cars. Ben gave Izzy and Oliver a thumbs-up as they hurried down the driveway.

When they got to the Bellwood Theater, the manager, looking relieved, met them out front and escorted Uncle Henderson backstage. People were beginning to trickle into the auditorium, but Izzy and her family stayed in the lobby, watching the audience arrive. They had reserved seats up front, but they were far too nervous to sit down until they absolutely had to.

Even though Izzy had known that Cookie and Pauline were coming, she was still happy to see them arrive with Pauline's parents. The adults went over to talk to her mother and Michael, and the two girls gave Izzy a tentative wave from across the room. *Really?*

"Why don't your friends come over here?" Oliver asked as he waved to them.

"They're afraid of Ben," Izzy said.

"I thought you told them I wasn't a serial killer after all," Ben said, grinning.

"I guess they don't believe me." Izzy motioned to her friends to come closer. If they were going to keep being her friends, they'd have to stop acting so ridiculous.

Cookie grabbed Pauline's arm, and the two of them approached cautiously. "Hey, Izzy," Pauline said. "Hi, Oliver. I can't wait to hear your dad."

Cookie's hand went straight to Izzy's hair. "Oh my God, you had it cut again. And I love this color! What's it called?"

"Vivid Violet," Izzy said.

"It's really pretty," Pauline told her. "I wish I had the nerve to dye mine."

"Thanks. Ben did it for me yesterday."

Both girls fluttered their eyelids and dared to look up at Ben.

"I guess you haven't actually met Ben," Izzy said. "If it weren't for him, Uncle Henderson probably wouldn't even have showed up here tonight."

Ben shrugged humbly. "So, which one of you is Cookie?"

Cookie raised her hand halfway, like a shy first grader in need of a bathroom break.

"Then you must be Pauline," he said. "I've heard all about you two."

"You have?" Pauline said, looking worried. "We're not really that bad!"

"Pauline!" Cookie gave her a little shove, and they both giggled and relaxed a little. "Do you really cut Izzy's hair?" Cookie dared to ask, her eyes big and round.

"I do," he said.

Izzy laughed. "Now they'll want you to cut *their* hair."

Cookie actually blushed, which Izzy had never

seen before. "Pauline's maybe, but I'm *never* cutting my hair." She threw her head back so her curls danced on her shoulders.

Ben tilted his head and gave her a sideways inspection. "Really? It would look better a few inches shorter."

Izzy could tell Cookie wasn't sure if he was joking or not. She laughed nervously and pulled on Pauline's arm. "We should go get seats," she said. Ben gave them a little wave as they disappeared into the theater.

"I can't believe you insulted her hair!" Izzy said. "She thinks she's one audition away from a shampoo commercial."

He laughed, as he did a lot these days. "She needs a better goal in life anyway."

"Izzy!" Her mother ran up and thrust her cell phone at her. "Your dad wants to talk to you. He's got big news!"

A storm swirled in Izzy's stomach. From the look of excitement on her mother's face, she was pretty sure she knew why her father was calling, and she didn't really want to hear his news. When she'd visited him last month, they'd had fun, almost as much fun as when he'd lived with her. She'd done her comedy routine for him, and he'd laughed so hard he started hiccupping. But now things were going to change. Her mother looked at her expectantly and held out the phone. *Rise to the occasion, Izzy.* She sighed and took the phone.

"Hello."

"Izzy, I've got good news! Your baby brother came two weeks early! He arrived about an hour ago, and he's a big, healthy guy with great lungs."

Had she ever heard her dad sound this happy? She didn't think so. "Wow," she said without a trace of enthusiasm. "Great."

"We're naming him Christopher. Christopher Shepherd. Do you like that name?"

"Sure. I guess." What did she care?

"I can't wait for you to come into town and meet him," her dad said. "Maybe over Christmas break—"

"I'm busy over the break," she said quickly. "We've got plans with Uncle Hen and Oliver and Michael and Ben. We're all going to this place in Vermont." Michael was excited about teaching her mother to ski, but Izzy intended to sit in front of a fireplace and drink cocoa.

"Oh, okay." He sounded disappointed, but he didn't give up. "Maybe just a weekend, then. I'll come out and get you. What do you think?"

Izzy thought it was a bad idea. Her father probably just wanted her to babysit so he and Emily could go out someplace. Or maybe he wanted to brag to her about what a terrific kid this new one was. She wasn't going to waste her vacation on *that*.

But then she looked up and saw that Ben had lifted Oliver onto his shoulders, and she remembered that change wasn't *always* a bad thing. Izzy's heart cracked open a little bit. And when it opened this time, her new baby brother slipped in. Like Ben had said, he might need her.

"Maybe I can," she said. "I'd like to see . . . Christopher."

"That's great, Izzy. We'll make plans. I have to go now, but we'll talk soon."

"Okay."

Her dad hesitated for a second and then he said, "Bye, Izzy. I love you." And then he was gone, before she could decide whether to say she loved him back.

"You okay, Iz?" Ben was beside her, Oliver still riding on his shoulders.

"I guess."

"You got another brother?" he asked.

"Yeah."

"Lucky you. A girl can never have too many of those."

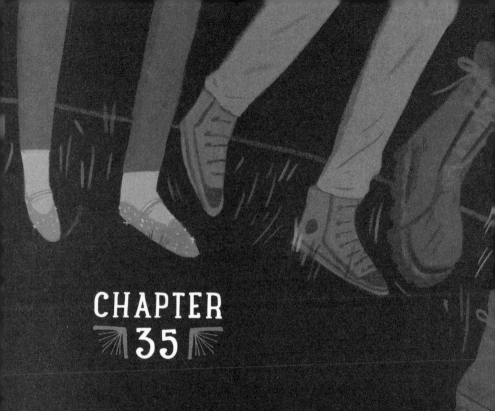

CHAPTER
35

Before long the lobby was packed. Izzy was shocked that so many people had come to hear her uncle play. Even Oliver's friend Suzanne and her not-yet-divorced parents came. They gripped her hands tightly as she walked between them like a captive, but Izzy could tell by the way she tossed her pigtails that she wouldn't be a prisoner for long.

Michael's voice suddenly cut through the other lobby noise. "What's *he* doing here?"

By the time Izzy turned around, Oliver had seen him and was flying over. "Look, Ben! It's your uncle!"

"Uncle Steve!" Ben said. Izzy followed them over to where the shaggy-haired giant stood just inside the door, looking a little out of place. The three of them formed a protective fence around Uncle Steve, even though it was obvious that Michael could break through it.

Ben shook his uncle's hand, but Uncle Steve pulled him into a hug. "Hey, I miss you, kiddo, you and your little buddies here. If this is the only way I can hang out with you, I'm willing to listen to a little guitar playing."

Michael was on top of them by then. "Didn't I ask you not to contact Ben anymore? Why are you here?" His face was bright red.

"This is a public place," Steve said. "I guess I can come to a concert if I want to."

"You didn't just happen to come here," Michael said. "You knew we'd be here. I don't like this at all."

Uncle Steve pulled his shoulders back and looked down at Michael. "Well, I don't really give a damn if you like it or not. This boy is my sister's child, and I have a right to see him if I want to."

"No, you don't. You've forfeited that right by your atrocious behavior—"

"Look," Uncle Steve interrupted, "I know you're mad at my sister, and you probably have a right to be. But it's not fair to keep me and Ben apart—

he's the only family I've got around here. Okay, I let him get some tattoos, and I taught him to drive a car when I probably shouldn't have. Hell, Mike, I never had any kids—I'm still a big kid myself, and I know I don't always make the right decisions. I'm sorry. But it doesn't make me a terrible guy, and you know it."

Michael was quiet, though Izzy could see the words he wasn't saying chasing each other around in his head. Izzy's mother came up behind him and put a hand on his arm.

"We should probably go in now," she said. "It'll be starting soon."

Michael sputtered out his thoughts. "There have to be rules, Steve. You can't let Ben do whatever he wants to do. I'm his *father*, do you understand that?"

Ben's uncle nodded. "I do. And I'll do my best to follow your rules. Just don't make 'em impossible."

"We'll discuss this later," Michael said. "When we aren't in public."

"Fine with me," Uncle Steve said, grinning at Ben.

"There's an extra seat in the front row, by us," Oliver said. "You should sit there." He grabbed Uncle Steve's hand and pulled him toward the entrance.

The rest of them fell in behind, Michael huffing

and snorting. Izzy heard her mother tell him, "It's okay, Michael. We'll figure it out."

And then they were in their seats, Oliver sandwiched between Izzy and Ben, bouncing nervously. The lights had gone down, and the audience was quiet. The manager came out onstage, and for a minute Izzy got scared. Was he going to say Uncle Henderson didn't want to play? Was he going to say he'd run out the back door and couldn't be found? But no, he stepped up to the microphone and said quietly, "This evening the Bellwood Theater is honored to present one of our favorite performers, the very talented . . . Henderson Hook."

Applause echoed through the auditorium. Izzy wondered if everyone here knew why Uncle Hen hadn't played a concert in six months. She figured they probably did.

Oliver jumped to his feet as Uncle Henderson walked out from the wings and perched on a high stool in the middle of the stage, his guitar balanced on one knee. He didn't look up right away, but strummed quietly until the clapping subsided. Then he fiddled with the microphone until it was at the right height. He looked around the big room and gave them a very small smile. No one moved, at least not in Izzy's row. They leaned forward and waited until Uncle Hen's voice broke the silence.

"I'd like to dedicate this first song to three

very important people," Uncle Henderson said. "My son, Oliver Hook; my niece, Izzy Shepherd; and my new friend, Ben Gustino." He looked right out at the three of them. "I owe them everything."

He began to sing, quietly at first, and then with his full, beautiful voice. Soon the words rang out over the auditorium. "Be always tender," he reminded the audience, and you could tell that everyone in that room understood just what he meant.

Izzy certainly did. She closed her eyes and let her heart rise to the occasion.

THE END

Acknowledgments

My writing has been sustained throughout the years by so many writer friends, particularly those in my two critique groups. Many thanks to Patty MacLachlan, Jane Yolen, Lesléa Newman, Ann Turner, Barbara Diamond Goldin, Corinne Demas, Nancy Werlin, Pat Lowery Collins, Lisa Papademetriou, Liza Ketchum, and Toni Buzzeo. I also depend on the advice and friendship of Elise Broach, Chris Tebbetts, Heather Knight Richard, Jeannine Atkins, and Lisa Yee.

As always, I thank the Fine Arts Work Center in Provincetown, Massachusetts, and the Kindling Words writing retreat for years of support and fellowship.

You would not be holding this book in your hands if not for the guidance and encouragement I've received from editors Yolanda Scott and Karen Boss. To all the other creative minds at Charlesbridge, particularly Donna Spurlock and Mel Schuit in marketing and copyeditor extraordinaire Josette Haddad, thank you so much. And of course, my constant gratitude goes to Ginger Knowlton: agent, advocate, and friend for more than twenty years.